PERSISTENCE PAYS

Kristal Ryan

A KISMET® Romance

METEOR PUBLISHING CORPORATION
Bensalem, Pennsylvania

To Judith Duncan, who brought us together, nursed us along and provided us with immeasurable support—and who taught us never to use cliches. We apologize, but sometimes they are a necessity, because, Judith—we couldn't have done it without you.

Also to our other support systems: Krissee Beaton, Fred Beaton, and the Hopf Menagerie.

KRISTAL RYAN

Kristal Ryan is the pseudonym of the Canadian writing team of Darlene Beaton-Harris and Grace Panko. Darlene was born in New Brunswick and raised on a train. She lives with a Clearasil kid, a neurotic black cat and an aging head-banger. Grace was born in Alberta and raised rather mundanely in a regular house. She lives with a sane but often harried husband, an aging arthritic cat and three rambunctious sons.

ONE

Katie O'Brien stared out the window of Al's Pizza Haven and tried, without success, to raise a breeze by fanning her face with a limp paper napkin. She wasn't exactly ignoring the two men sitting on the other side of the small table; it was just that the sweltering heat made it hard for her to concentrate on more than one thing at a time.

Outside, the blistering hundred-degree temperature did little to discourage the regular army of flamboyant would-be stars from manning their posts in front of nearly every doorway along Hollywood Boulevard. Everything from Madonna look–alikes to Bon Jovi clones normally strutted their perfected stuff in hopes of discovery and instant fame, but today their movements were lethargic and severely affected by the stale, muggy air.

Inside, the atmosphere was even worse. The air conditioner had died, and heat radiated from the kitchen in persistent waves of garlic, salami, and tomato sauce that on any normal day would stimulate the appetite. Today the heavy blend of smells did anything but. Katie supposed she should be grateful that the refrigerator still worked. At least the Coke was cold and kicked all the way down.

Sal Domina reluctantly set his frosty glass on the red-checkered tablecloth, wadded up his napkin, and wiped at the trickles of sweat gathered in the fold of his double chin. He cast a questioning glance at Katie's father, Charlie O'Brien, before heaving a melodramatic sigh in Katie's direction. "So . . . now I'm short a photographer, and I don't know what I'm gonna do. Lenn's a first-class reporter, but when it comes to taking a good picture, well . . ." He rolled his eyes toward the white stucco ceiling. "I'm sunk. *Sunk*."

Katie didn't respond. She was lost in the arrogant antics of a maharajah impersonator strolling in front of the building across the street. She vaguely wondered if there was any money in dressing in funny clothes. If she didn't find a job soon she just might be desperate enough to give it a try.

"Ask her," Charlie whispered frantically at his old boyhood crony.

"I'm working on it," Sal muttered back. "I can't just—"

"Now, Sal. She's not going to do it if you don't ask."

"What's the difference? She's not listening anyway. Look at her."

At some vague level Katie could hear the murmur between Sal and her father, but she was too wrapped up in her own problems to wonder what they were up to this time. The bottom had fallen out of her professional world, and where she had once known security, she now had uncertainty. She loathed the idea of having to start over again. It frightened her. Change frightened her. On the other hand, she liked to eat. Which was why she was sweating out the lunch hour with her father and Sal. She couldn't turn down a free meal, but she wished they had picked a place where the air conditioning worked.

"So, what do you think, Katie?" Sal's dark-brown eyes were alert with anticipation.

Katie blinked and met his gaze. "About what?"

"I told you she wasn't listening." He slumped back in his chair with a shrug of defeat. "Maybe this isn't such a good time to bring it up."

"Don't be ridiculous," Charlie hissed. "It's as good a time as any. Ask her again."

Katie flicked a suspicious glance from one man to the other. They were up to something, this pair of aging potbellied bandits. In their circle of family and friends they were known as Butch Cassidy and the Sundance Kid, and with good reason. They were always up to some dumb trick or other, in spite of the fact that both were in their fifties and old enough to know better.

The two of them had been raising hell for a long time. As children, they had attended the same parochial boys' school and, according to Grandma O'Brien, had totally terrorized the nuns. Forty-odd years of friendship might have mellowed them some, but even today, when they were in the same room, anyone with half a brain in their head would be wise to stand with his back to the wall. And right now, Katie wondered if she should have chosen a safer seat.

"What are you two talking about?" She shouldn't have asked. She knew better.

Sal cleared his throat. "You must have heard that Daryl, the photographer who's been working with Lenn, has quit and moved to Hawaii?"

"Of course," she said, somewhat warily. "Dad must've mentioned it at least twenty times in the last three days. What's that got to do with anything?"

"Sal needs a replacement for Daryl," Charlie supplied, "and we both thought of you."

It finally dawned on her that this lunch wasn't free after all. It was a setup. A cunning little conspiracy cooked up by two old pros to con her into taking a job they knew she wouldn't want. First of all, she wasn't a news photographer. She photographed babies and weddings, for Pete's sake. True, right now she wasn't doing even that since the studio where she had worked had gone belly-up. Her boss—her ex-boss, that is—had siphoned all the profits onto the tables at Vegas, but she knew she'd eventually find a place that would let her take the nice friendly little pictures she was used to taking. She sure didn't want to work as a news photographer for Sal's family-owned daily.

It wasn't that she couldn't handle the job. After all, her training had covered photojournalism as well as portrait photography. She didn't want to hare around town snapping photos of things that didn't have the least intention of posing cooperatively—and she sure didn't want to do it with Lenn Domina. No matter how desperate she was for employment, she wasn't in so sorry a state that she would consent to work with that insensitive excuse for a human being. As a matter of fact, ever since she had learned that

Sal's oldest son had returned to Los Angeles two months ago, she had been going out of her way to avoid running into him.

"No." She fixed Sal with a hard, uncompromising glare.

"Why not?" her father inquired innocently, as if he hadn't been around to witness the animosity that had sizzled between Lenn and her while they were growing up.

How can I phrase this diplomatically? she wondered for the briefest second before deciding diplomacy be damned. "Because I don't want to work with Lenn, that's why not. I *would* be working with him if I was nuts enough to accept this offer, wouldn't I?"

"Well . . . yes, but I think you're being a little unfair. Lenn's not like he used to be." Sal defended his son with a pained expression. "He's still a little unconventional maybe, but—"

"Unconventional, my foot. I'd make book that Daryl would still be working at *Newsprobe* if you hadn't teamed him with Lenn, and if a professional news photographer couldn't stand working with him, you can't expect me to hack it." Katie stabbed her fork into the rapidly wilting lettuce in her salad. It was a shame really. She *could* use the job. If only she didn't have to work with Lenn. She stopped her fork halfway to her mouth. "Wait a minute, Sal. You've got a whole staff of photographers. Why don't you get one of your stringers to work with Lenn? I could maybe help out by taking up some of the slack." *And I wouldn't have to work with Lenn.* Katie smiled at the brilliance of her plan.

Sal glanced desperately at Charlie.

Charlie swallowed hard. "Uh, they're all assigned. Isn't that right Sal?"

"Yeah, that's it. I mean, that's right. They're all assigned."

"Then reassign one," Katie suggested.

Sal flicked his wadded-up napkin with one pudgy finger. "Can't. I uh, you see, I have this policy." He looked over at Charlie, whose head was bobbing up and down encouragingly. "Yeah, I don't like to break up a successful team, and all my other photographers are already assigned to other reporters."

Katie sighed. Something stunk to high heaven here. She was positive Sal was stringing her a line. Well, she wasn't biting. More than likely the truth was that none of the other photographers wanted to work with Lenn. And she didn't blame them. Neither did she. "Then run an ad in the classifieds. If you're lucky, some poor unsuspecting soul out there won't have heard about Lenn and will apply for the job. I certainly don't want it."

"Now, Katie, have a little compassion. Sal needs someone right away." Charlie leaned solicitously toward his daughter. "Even if he runs an ad, it could take weeks before anyone fills the bill. Lenn can't possibly cover his stories alone. He's a lousy photographer, but we all know how great you are. Besides, you're out of a job just when Sal needs a photographer. I'll bet it's fate. How can you let down someone who's been like family all your life?"

Fatherly pressure was Charlie's specialty. He was trying to make her feel guilty. They both were, with their soulful, sweaty gazes. Well, it wasn't going to work. She could be as stubborn as they were. Tuning them out, she deliberately turned her attention to the scene outside the window. There was no way she could work with Lenn Domina.

Memories slammed into her brain—memories of the rotten stunts he had pulled on her in those years before he left to live with his grandparents in Italy. Her blood still roiled over the events of that last summer. The Dominas and the O'Briens had decided to go camping in the hills of Colorado for a month. *It'll be great for the kids!* Sal had declared. *The fresh mountain air will do us all a world of good!* Charles had agreed.

It had been the worst damned summer of Katie's life. Roughing it had never been her style. And rough it was. They had crammed twelve—count 'em, twelve!—people into a puny little cabin way out in the middle of some stupid forest where no one had ever gone before. No one but the fool who had built the century-old shack. There had been Charlie and Vanessa O'Brien; Katie and her brother Chris; Salvatore and Giovanna Domina and their clan—Lenn, who was fourteen then; Tony; Maria; Angie; Benny and Sylvia. Crowded was an understatement. Needless to say, the kids bunked down in sleeping bags while their elders shared the only bedroom. Katie hadn't minded that, and she hadn't minded spending the first week of this so-called vacation cleaning out and fixing up the old cabin. She could handle a chore or two.

What she could not handle was Lenn Domina. Just before school had let out Katie had developed her first crush. It was just her luck that her burgeoning feelings were directed at her black-eyed tormentor— the boy who spent every waking moment of that summer thinking up ways to make her life unbearable. The spiders in the basin she washed in each morning were bad enough, but when he learned of her phobia about snakes, he slipped one into her sleeping bag. Nothing could have horrified her more than the feel of that slithering creature as it coiled itself around her legs. Dear God, she could still feel it.

But the crunch of the matter went deeper than an endless stock of tricks. What Lenn had really done all those years ago was undermine her self-esteem. He had always been so self-assured, so street-wise—all those things that separated the in crowd from those who remained on the outside looking in.

Katie had been on the outside. The one who always had her homework done on time. The one who refused to smoke cigarettes behind the little gray building in the park. She had been an Orphan Annie with homely freckles, unsightly red hair that refused to flatten even when she ironed it, and a wide gap between her two front teeth that didn't close until she was seventeen. She hated her looks. She had hated them so vehemently she couldn't bear to look in a mirror.

And true to form, once Lenn discovered her crush on him, he had used her feelings as further ammunition in his war of torment. Not only did he continue with his idiotic stunts, but he augmented his campaign by attacking her character, her looks. He made cracks about her hair, claiming it glowed in the dark and kept him awake. He taunted her at meals, saying she was the only one there who didn't need to part her teeth to use a straw.

Oh, she got over him in record time on that vacation, but she never got over the pain of having been rejected and humiliated by the first boy she'd cared for. And that, she admitted, was the real root of her aversion to Lenn Domina.

Now Sal wanted her to work with him. She could feel the drilling looks from two pairs of puppy-dog eyes and tried to ignore the disconcerting hole forming in the side of her neck. She couldn't.

"Don't keep staring at me as if I'm going to change my mind. I'm not."

"But, Katie, Lenn's changed," Charlie insisted. "He's not the same boy you used to know. He's more mature and, uh, responsible, and uh, dammit, Sal—help me out here, will you?"

Sal coughed. "Uh . . . yeah. He's changed. He really has. Uh, well, maybe he is still a little moody, but it's nothing you couldn't adjust to if you tr—"

"*You* adjust to him," Katie cut in dryly. "I'm staying as far away from him as I can."

Turning toward Charlie, Sal shrugged his shoulders and lifted his eyebrows. Katie hoped it meant he was ready to give up.

"But, Katie, what about the challenge?" Charlie O'Brien *never* gave up. "You're too good a photographer to spend your life taking pictures of snottynosed little kids. Just think, you could take pictures that would be on the front page of a newspaper. You could—"

"I don't want to." In spite of her refusal, Katie felt a little twinge. A tiny part of her admitted that wasn't entirely the truth. She did want to do something more with her life than take pictures of fussy babies who wasted half a roll of film with drooling squalls before relinquishing the one small smile that filled a successful frame. Katie stirred the last limp green leaf in the oil and vinegar separating in the bottom of her bowl. The offer was really tempting. Working with Lenn was not. Hold it, hadn't she heard somewhere that . . .

"Um, not that I care, but is Lenn planning to stay in L.A. permanently? I was under the impression he was only going to cover a few stories for your paper, then move on again." Katie absently swallowed the last bite of her salad. Maybe she could hack it if it was short term. Very short term.

"It's hard to say what his plans are." A flash of pain darkened Sal's brown eyes. "But as Charlie said, he's changed, Katie. Enough that I think he might stick around this time—if he finds a good reason to."

She saw her hope of the job being a short-term possibility slip away. "Look, Sal, I understand that you want Lenn to live here permanently." And she did. She might hate the son, but she loved the father. It was pretty obvious Sal had missed Lenn during the years he'd been away. Fighting against her natural sympathy, she sucked in a breath of resolve. "I can't help you. You must know that Lenn and I could never work together."

"No, I don't. Lenn's not a teenager anymore."

"Sal's right," Charlie jumped in. "You're both adults now. There's no reason you can't work together."

They were pulling out all the stops. Appealing to her maturity. Hah! It still wasn't going to work. Lenn Domina was the type of person who would never grow up no matter how old he got. Katie gathered up her purse.

"Please," Sal spoke in desperation. "Don't leave. There's no one I can get on such short notice."

She pushed her chair away from the table. "Sal, I hardly believe your paper will fold without me."

"Katie." Charlie reached over and tugged at her arm. "Sal was depending on you, you know."

"Yeah, I was," Sal agreed with a vigorous nod, "and I can't believe that you, of all people, would let me down this way. Wasn't it me who took you to the dentist when Charlie was away on business—and held your hand through the whole ordeal? Wasn't it me who bought you your first two-wheeler—and taught you how to ride it? Wasn't it—"

"All right already! You've made your point." She heaved a sigh of concession, which was followed by a long silence shared by all three. Even as she spoke, she knew she would regret the words she blurted out. "Heaven help me, but when do you want me to start?"

"Tomorrow?" Sal's grin closely resembled that of a man who had just found out he'd won a million-dollar lottery.

"Okay." Katie expelled a puff of disgusted air. "Wait. On second thought, make that Monday. I'm going to need the weekend to get used to the idea. And Sal, you've got to promise me one thing. Promise it'll only be until you find a replacement, because there's no way on God's green earth that I'm going to work with Lenn on a permanent basis."

"I promise."

Katie raised one very skeptical eyebrow.

"He promises," her father quickly verified.

* * *

The rubber soles of Lenn Domina's sneakers slapped against the serviceable tiles stretching along the corridor leading to the darkroom. It was bad enough that Sal was insisting on this crazy new policy of assigning him a permanent photographer. But a woman! How could he do this to him? After more than three decades in the newspaper business, the old man was finally losing his marbles. A woman couldn't endure the physical abuse that went hand in hand with the type of stories he usually covered. Lord, he could imagine what would've happened if he'd had a woman with him when he covered that gang war last month. Even Daryl hadn't escaped unscathed; he'd ended up with a couple of bruised ribs trying to save his camera—a wasted effort, though he did manage to salvage the film. And he sure didn't intend dragging a woman along when he interviewed pimps or drug dealers. Where the hell were Sal's brains when he hired her?

"At least meet her before you judge. She's down in the darkroom. Give her a chance, Lenn." He could still hear Pop's words echoing in his ears. Well, he'd give her a chance all right. A chance to change her mind and get out while the getting was good—before she got hurt. Lenn picked up his pace, adding an extra measure of determination to each of his strides. He was going to be firm. Firm but not chauvinistic. The last thing he needed was an irate female on his hands. He hadn't been able to talk any sense into his father, but maybe, just maybe, this dame might have half a head on her shoulders, and when he explained the dangers of the job and the stamina she'd need, she would take her camera and leave. It was for her own good. Surely she would see that. Yeah, and maybe he'd wake up in the morning and find out peace had been declared throughout the universe.

Damn, he wished he hadn't been so ticked off at his old man that he hadn't even found out her name. It would have given him an edge. Lenn ground a heel into the tile and swung around the last corner. A soft red glow spilled onto the floor of the corridor. Great! He gave a snort of disgust. What kind of photographer left the door open when the safelight was on? So much for expecting to appeal to her intelligence. She obviously didn't have any.

Shaking his head, he slipped inside the door and waited a moment for his eyes to adjust to the dim red light. If World War III was about to break out he wanted to see who the enemy was. Gradually, in the far corner of the room, a rather petite female form came into focus. She was bent over at an almost perfect forty-five-degree angle with a very delightful bottom in the air, legs slightly apart, and if the flicker of the flashlight in her hand was any indication, she was obviously searching for something in the lower cupboard. Somewhere in the back of his mind, the incongruity of someone using a flashlight in a safelit darkroom registered, but his predatory streak was too strong for him to worry about logistics at the moment. There was something about a sight like this that could knock the wind out of even Arnold Schwarzenegger. And if it didn't, he wasn't as red-blooded as he appeared in all those movies.

A slow grin of appreciation grew across Lenn's face. Lord, he was tempted to sidle over and run a hand over the smooth, tightened material that, given her position, was barely covering the essentials. He jammed his hands into the back pockets of his jeans. Damn, if that soft red glow didn't add to the sensuality of her pose. Lenn swallowed the lump gathering in his Adam's apple. She might have one of the all-time great behinds, but he still had no intention of working with her. Of course, there sure wasn't any harm in enjoying the view.

"Whatever you're looking for down there, I hope it takes you at least another ten minutes to find it."

Startled by the unexpected voice, Katie straightened suddenly, whacking her head against an upper cupboard door. Muttering a few choice words under her breath, she wheeled around to glare at the intruder. "Don't you know better than to sneak up on a person? You almost gave me a heart att—" Her jaw dropped. Lenn Domina? The dark taunting eyes were undeniably his, but . . .

"Katie?" Lenn's forehead wrinkled his brows into a V. "Katie O'Brien. Is that you?"

Good Lord, Katie thought, the teenage imitation of the Italian stud had grown into the real thing. And it still got to her. He'd always been too good-looking for his own good, but there'd be skating in hell before she'd let *him* know that. She masked her astonishment under a cool, unbending gaze of disinterest. "Of course, it's me. Who else would be living in my body?"

"Well, from what I can make out, the coloring is familiar." Lenn stepped back to check out every inch of her anatomy. "But are you sure that's your body? The design seems to have changed."

Katie pressed her lips in a line and turned back to the cupboard. *One . . . two . . . three . . .* She was not going to let him get to her. *Four . . . five . . .*

six . . . Not even if she had to count to one bloody hundred. Pretend he isn't there. Find a stinking bulb and get some decent light in the room. He looked too much like the devil he was in the red glow that washed over his disgustingly fit body.

"Wouldn't it be easier to find what you're looking for if you turned on the regular light? You don't seem to be developing anything."

Condescending bastard. Katie turned and glared pointedly at the naked socket over his head. Lenn flicked a glance upward.

"Hey," he snapped his fingers, "I'll bet you're looking for a bulb."

"Well, I'll give you one thing, Domina. You're as quick as ever."

Lenn sauntered over to the cupboard and reached over Katie's head. Extracting a bulb from a carton sitting out in plain view, he casually slung a chair beneath the empty socket. With lithe economy, he climbed up and replaced the fixture.

It wasn't her fault she was too short to see the top of the cabinet. Katie clicked off the flashlight and slapped it on the counter, quickly flipping the switch that turned off the safelight and returned the room to normal visibility. She felt a tiny bit safer.

Lenn shunted the chair back into the corner and leaned a jeaned hip against the counter. Folding his arms across his chest, he studied her for what seemed like an excessively long time. *So this is what a bug under a microscope feels like,* Katie thought. Lenn always did have the knack of making her feel uncomfortable. She resisted the urge to squirm.

"Let me get this straight." Lenn shook his head in disbelief. "*You're* Daryl's replacement?"

"That's right," Katie replied with a slightly indignant, ladylike sniff. "Do you have a problem with that?" And before he got the chance to slide in a dig of his own, she added, "Of course you would, knowing that old-world attitude of yours."

"Hey, I resent that. How can you say a thing like that when you haven't seen me in years?" Lenn shifted his position slightly, causing the denim covering his hips to tighten further. "Especially when I was trying to be so nice."

"Don't try that *nice* stuff on me, Lenn." Katie stubbornly held his gaze. It wasn't easy. Those jeans of his fit like the skin of a snake. Luckily, the thought of snakes strengthened her resolve. "You weren't being nice; you were trying to figure out how to zero in on me. I've heard about you and your exploits over the years. This is going to be a professional arrangement. Nothing more. Understand?"

"No. I don't. What are you talking about?"

"From what I understand, you'd actively pursue an orangutan if it had a skirt on."

Much to her surprise, he grinned. "If it had a backside like yours, I might consider it."

"As I said, I've heard all about you."

"Oh, come on, Katie. Lighten up. I'm willing to bury the hatchet if you are."

"Fat chance," Katie muttered as she stepped around him and headed toward the door. She'd like to bury it all right. Right between his eyes.

Lenn strolled out behind her, still checking out the rear view, but smart enough not to comment again. Katie surprised him; not only had she physically matured, but her character had undergone a distinctive change. She certainly wasn't the mouse who'd cowered at his every taunt. No, sir. She'd become pretty sharp with her comebacks. Damn, if he didn't kind of like that sassy streak in her. This Katie didn't take off with her tail between her legs like she used to. Maybe working with her wouldn't be so bad after all. She was kind of small, though—didn't look as if she could fight her way through a wet paper napkin.

"For Pete's sake." Katie stopped and glared over her shoulder. "Would you at least walk beside me? I don't trust you behind my back."

Lenn flashed a set of impossibly white teeth. "God, you look great. What happened?"

"What do you mean, what happened? Nothing happened. I grew up, that's all."

"Did you ever! Last time I saw you, you were flat-chested and covered with freckles, and you had hipbones I could hang a hat on." He laughed softly.

Why did he have to bring that up? It was one memory she'd just as soon forget. Her friends had been with her the day Lenn decided it would be funny to sneak up behind her and try to hang his black felt hat on her hipbone. She had cried all the way home, and when she recounted the incident to her father, he had initially burst into peals of mirth. After seeing her stricken face, however, he reassured her that all the O'Brien women looked like walking skeletons until they reached puberty when they filled out in all the right places. Katie hadn't believed him at the time. Nothing could have eased the hot, red sting of humiliation. Now that her hips were quite adequately padded, maybe a little too much so, she could see some humor in the incident—not much, but some.

It had taken her long agonizing years to accept and

be comfortable with her appearance after all the insults Lenn had tossed her way. And now that she had, she was not going to listen to Lenn bait her again. He'd been known to do exactly that more than once. She remembered well enough how he could turn on her like a cobra—seemingly cool and placid one moment, then mean and hurtful the next. That's the way he was. And she wasn't taking anyone's word that he had changed, least of all Charlie's or Sal's.

Katie deliberately changed the subject. "So, what brought you back to Los Angeles?"

The nostalgic smile he had been wearing slowly receded, leaving in its wake a solemn expression that revealed little. "I don't really know," he shrugged thoughtfully. "Let's just say I've got some unfinished business to take care of and let it go at that."

Katie pushed her tongue to the roof of her mouth, irritated at his deliberately vague reply. "Very expertly done, Lenn." She could feel the *Whaddaya mean?* glare burning the side of her face and added, "You always were a pro at blurting out statements that mean virtually nothing at all."

"They would if you thought about them."

"Yeah," she said, stopping abruptly to stare up at him expressionlessly, "but maybe I'm not interested enough to bother."

Lenn's dark eyes snapped. She had pinched a nerve. And she was glad.

"Aren't you?" Lenn stalked down the corridor and slammed open the swinging doors that led into the office. He turned and glared at her. "Are you coming or not?"

He kept a level eye on her as she closed the gap

between them. She deliberately took her sweet old time, stubbornly holding his gaze. He was sulking because she refused to bite on the line he was dangling in her face. As she reached him, she heaved a great sigh. "Okay. I'll humor you this time. What unfinished business did you come to take care of? And make it simple, okay? I'm not in the mood to dig."

"I wouldn't tell you now if my life depended on it."

"See, I knew you were baiting me."

"It's not that," he grumbled disgustedly. "You wouldn't understand. And not because you couldn't. You just wouldn't try."

"Please," she moaned dramatically. "Stop. I'm practically in tears. This is *sooo* heart-wrenching."

"Can it, Katie." Lenn stepped into the office where a dozen or so reporters hunched over video display terminals. Katie skirted the door he'd deliberately let swing in her face. A few heads raised briefly, then the reporters bent back over their keyboards. Lenn spoke in a quiet voice as he ushered her toward his desk. "You've always believed only what you wanted to, just like most people. You couldn't see the value in anything I did if it hit you in the face. Which is why I won't bother trying." Lenn pulled a second chair up to his desk and folded his sturdy frame into the seat behind it. "Park it."

Katie parked it, biting her lip to keep from retorting. Any comment she might be tempted to make would start an argument, she knew, and she wasn't in the mood for one. Her head still stung from the crack she'd taken, and she could feel a zinger of a headache coming on.

"So." She moistened her lips and averted her eyes to scan the room. "What happens around here, anyway?"

Aw crap, this was even worse than he had expected. She didn't have a clue about what went on in a newspaper office. Which made it unlikely she knew what to expect in the field. Well, there it was—the perfect out. All he had to do was describe a few of the graphic details involved in the job and she'd be running to Pop, begging out of the job. He had some pretty good reasons why he didn't want to work with a woman, and Katie sure in hell was a woman. His dark eyes took a tour of her body, paused at her well-toned calves, then reversed course to where she was tugging at the hem of her short skirt. He did enjoy making her squirm. He always had, only now it was for a very different reason. It might be fun to keep her around just to keep a hand in. No, come to think of it, he'd be smarter to keep his hands to himself.

"You mean Pop didn't tell you anything about the kinds of stories I cover?" Irritated at the direction of his thoughts, Lenn spoke more sharply than he had intended.

"Nope, not a thing. I have no idea what I'm getting into." Katie's cool green eyes challenged him to make something of her inexperience. "I'm doing this as a favor for your father. He said you needed someone immediately."

"I do." Lenn knew he should be storming into Sal's office this very minute, demanding he find someone else. Katie's lack of experience gave him the justification he needed. He slouched deeper into his chair. "But he should have known better than to pair me up with a woman . . . Hold it, before you get defensive.'' She prickled exactly as he expected. "I don't mean that in the way you think.'' The hell he didn't. "Things can be pretty rough out there. Are you prepared to stick your neck out for a few good shots?''

"I'll do what I have to. I made it through a childhood with you, didn't I? I can survive anything after that.''

He'd almost expected the first part of her answer, but not the barb that followed. Focusing on a worn spot on the knee of his jeans, he twirled a loose thread between his thumb and index finger. He remembered some of the pranks he had played on her when they were kids. With adult perspective, he suddenly realized that what an unthinking teenager considered funny might have been hurtful. Regret tightened in his chest. "I guess I could look out for you, if need be. Working with you can't be any worse than working with Daryl.''

Certain it had been the other way round as far as Daryl was concerned, Katie had a hard time biting back a comment, but she sure didn't want to precipitate another philosophical tirade. "I can look out for myself. I'm not exactly an invalid.''

"Honey, that sharp tongue won't do you a whole lot of good in a scrap.''

"I'll have to stay out of the way, then. Won't I?''

"Good,'' he nodded, his eyes darting downward to study her legs as she crossed them. "I wouldn't want anything happening to that delightful little body of yours.''

"Hah.''

"What! You don't think your body's delightful?''

"I don't think about it all that much."

"Well then, I'll have to think about it for both of us, and believe me, I don't think I'll have too much difficulty."

"For all the good it'll do you."

"Hmm, aren't you the cool one these days?" he taunted with a smile. "But that's okay. I enjoy a challenge now and then."

"A conquest, you mean."

"That, too. You know, if I'd known you'd grown into such an enticing woman, I'd have come back to L.A. years ago."

"Stuff it, Lenn. I'm not one of your flighty airheads." A *Cosmopolitan* beauty, Katie knew she was not. Orange hair might have made Lucille Ball immortal, but it hadn't won her any Oscars. Katie faced the fact that her nose was too thin and her lips too fat, and while she was evaluating herself, she had to admit her thighs were a tad too porky. However, no one was perfect, or for that matter, entirely pleased with what nature had given them, and she was no different. But she could smell a con job a mile away, and she was picking up the distinct odor of one right now. Losing patience, she spoke tersely. "Look around you, Lenn."

Insolently, he did, then casually returned his attention to her, waiting for elaboration.

"There are three other women in this room, not counting the ones across the hall. Why pick on me?"

"I've become a creature of habit." Lenn hooked an ankle across one knee. "I seem to be leaning toward things that are familiar to me these days. And I certainly think you fit that category."

"You?" she gaped. "A creature of habit? Get real.

The only habit you have is slithering out of the wood-work every so often to make everyone miserable.''

"People change."

"So I've been told." And a little too often, Katie decided. "I'll believe it when I see it."

"I want to be there to see the look on your face when you do." Lenn grinned.

The phone on the desk shrilled.

TWO

"Grab your camera, Red. We're on." Lenn's feet hit the floor before the receiver hit the cradle. Snatching up the green canvas bag containing his recorder, he zigzagged a path between the desks without even looking back to see if she was following.

A burst of adrenaline coursed through her veins. Katie dashed to Sal's office, where she'd left her camera bag. Without knocking, she wrenched open the door, grabbed the leather case, and scrambled after Lenn, not paying the slightest bit of attention to the startled looks on the faces of Sal and the reporter he had in his office. Lenn was at the end of the corridor before she caught up with him.

"Where are we going?" she puffed, thinking vaguely that she'd better start working out again. She was beginning to realize that she might need to be in better shape if she intended to keep up with Lenn Domina.

"A bunch of guys crossed the picket line at the

airport and all hell broke loose," he said brusquely as he headed toward the elevators.

"Anyone hurt?"

He shot her a quelling glance. "Of course people have been hurt. Why do you think we're heading out there?" Lenn jabbed impatiently at the elevator button.

"There's no need to be so sarcastic." Katie stomped into the elevator the minute the ancient doors lumbered open. She thought her question had been logical. He wasn't even trying to be civil. He knew she didn't have any experience at this sort of thing—the least he could do was give her a chance. But *nooo*, not Lenn. She, at least, was trying. She'd agreed to work with him, hadn't she? And she'd spent the whole weekend persuading herself that they could get along if they both tried. But that was the clincher. He had to try, too. Would he? Were Sal and her dad even a little bit right?

She sidestepped an inch and shot him a surreptitious glance. He was shifting restlessly from one leg to the other, ready to spring forward the moment the elevator stopped. She had to admit that the rebellion and defiance of his youth were no longer mirrored in those dark-brown eyes, but the emotion that was there now was just as intense and perhaps even more lethal.

"Why are you staring at me like that?" he growled.

Katie quickly snapped her eyes up to study the numerical dial above the antiquated doors. "No reason. We taking your car or mine?"

"Neither. I don't know about you, but I'm too

attached to mine to drive it into a riot. We'll take one of the staff vans."

The elevator doors barely lurched open before he caught her elbow and pulled her through, then raced her to the back parking lot toward a van with the *Newsprobe* logo splashed across the side. Lenn released her for a moment as he slid open the paneled door and tossed in his pack. When he reached for her again, Katie sidestepped the attempt and snapped acidly, "Would you please stop shoving me around. I'm quite capable of getting into a vehicle by myself."

"In that outfit? That skimpy little skirt's so tight I'm surprised you can move at all. And those heels . . . hell, you don't walk in them, you pussyfoot. If I hadn't hustled you along, you'd still be teetering out of the elevator." Lenn jumped into the van and slid into the driver's seat. "Well, come on. I've got a job to do. I don't have any time to waste on someone who doesn't have enough sense to dress for the job."

"Can it, Domina, there's nothing wrong with the way I dress." Katie hiked her skirt up a couple of inches and struggled into the van, cursing Lenn under her breath. It wasn't her fault that the van was so high and she was so short, but she had to concede that he might have just the tiniest point. She wasn't about to admit it, though.

"No, not if you want to flash your backside at anyone passing by. Why didn't you wear pants? You don't have any more sense than you did when you were ten." Lenn fired the ignition with a wrench of the key and jerked the van out of the parking space.

Katie fell the last few inches into the torn bucket

seat. "Bastard." The muttered word escaped between the teeth she was grinding together in an ineffectual effort to contain her temper.

"What did you say?" Lenn slammed on the brakes, nearly throwing her out of the seat. His eyes narrowed to glittering slits as he turned toward her.

"Nothing," Katie seethed, not about to give him the satisfaction of knowing he had made her lose her composure. "I thought you were in such an all-fired hurry. What are you waiting for?"

Lenn glared at her for a long, charged moment. When he finally spoke, his voice was low, gravelly, and deadly quiet. "I'm giving you one warning, Katie. Don't ever call me that again."

"Or you'll do what?" Katie challenged, defiantly clicking her seat belt closed. She didn't bother reminding him to fasten his. Let him kill himself.

Lenn didn't answer. He lifted his sneakered foot off the brake and pulled onto the traffic-congested street. They rode in silence until he turned the van onto the freeway. The ten minutes or so that had dragged by before he spoke again must have been enough time for him to cool down.

"Well, I'll say one thing for you, O'Brien—you're a lot gutsier than you used to be."

Katie stared straight ahead. She was not going to be drawn into another argument.

Lenn accepted her stubborn silence for all of five minutes. "Are you seeing anyone?"

Katie tried to maintain her resolve not to speak, but the thought that Lenn probably believed she wasn't capable of hanging on to a man was too much for her. "Not that it's any of your business, but, yeah, I am."

"You are?"

He didn't need to sound so incredulous.

"What's his name?"

"What's it to you?"

"I like to know the competition," he shrugged. "I kinda hoped the coast might be clear, but what the heck, I've already warned you that I like a challenge. How about dinner tonight?"

Her eyes stretched wide, she turned her head and stared. The utter gall of the man. "I'd rather eat dog food for a month than have dinner with you—and didn't I just tell you I was seeing someone?"

"Now, Katie," Lenn grinned, "you should know by now that a little thing like that's not going to stop me. I always get what I want."

"Not this time."

"We'll see."

"Lenn," she said through gritted teeth, "put a lid on it. Hasn't it occurred to you that I might not be interested in anything you say or do?"

"Ha. I know you better than that."

"So you'd like to think."

"So I know. Granted you have changed some. Everyone does, but I'd wager a month's earnings that you're still as curious as ever. You are, aren't you, Red?"

She'd ignored his earlier reference to her coloring, hoping he'd drop it when she didn't respond. She should have known better. He *never* let go and she couldn't stand it any longer. "Don't call me that. I didn't like it fifteen years ago, and I don't like it now!"

The corner of Lenn's mouth quirked distinctly as he shot a look into the mirror on Katie's side of the van before pulling onto the exit ramp. "Nice to know *some* things never change."

Right, she thought, and it's nice to know that some things *do*. Or is it?

An all-out war was in progress in front of the air terminal. Dozens of men and women were wrapped around each other, screaming obscenities and using anything they could get their hands on to clobber one another. Katie wasn't surprised the situation had gotten out of hand. The baggage handlers had been locked in a wage dispute for over a month.

After giving his recorder a cursory check, Lenn hopped up a curb to crane his tall frame even taller. "I think I see the head of the union in that bunch. I'm going to get myself a story. Keep your distance but get some shots." He plunged into the melee before Katie could retort that she couldn't do one and still manage the other.

She scanned the scene with more than a little trepidation. The area was scattered with police vehicles and ambulances. Flashing red lights reflected in the windows of nearby buildings, and riot-garbed officers were using night sticks to try to get the mob under control. Unsure whether she was drawn into the core of the human cyclone by the excitement, or hauled in by unseen forces, Katie suddenly found herself dodging clubs and broken pop bottles. After managing to snap a number of good close-ups of people snarling and baring their teeth like a pack of pit bulls, she tried her darnedest to squeeze her way back out and still protect her equipment, but some unknown hand kept yanking her back in, probably assuming she was on one side or the other. Nobody, she was certain, knew which was which. At one point she tried to reason with a captor but got cuffed in the mouth by a robust woman who had the southpaw of a Canadian lumberjack. Finally, she slid onto all fours and crawled out clutching her camera beneath her.

Lenn was nowhere to be seen. Katie bobbed and searched for an anxious few minutes before a rolling blue denim streak was hurled onto the asphalt. Face first. Lenn staggered to his feet, spitting dirt and checking to see if his nose was broken. Katie limped across the pavement on one broken heel, about to ask if he was okay, when she noticed the self-satisfied grin on his face.

"Damn, I got a good story, and I'd have gotten even more if those two burly apes hadn't nailed me." He finally noticed her ragged state. "What happened to you?"

She shrugged, glancing down at herself. "I got a little more involved than I expected. Can we get out of here now—*before* we get killed?"

"I suppose you'll want to go home and change," Lenn sighed with resignation.

"Yeah, well I guess so, eh? I certainly don't want anyone seeing me like this."

"I think you look kinda cute. In any case, you'll have to tolerate the humiliation for a while. You've got to get those pictures developed, and I need to get to a VDT before we can think about checking out for as long as it's likely to take you to change. Besides, you wouldn't need to if you'd dressed for the job in the first place."

He couldn't resist the I-told-you-so jibe, could he? Katie seethed as she hobbled after him. "Why don't you drop me off on the way, and I'll meet you back at the office,'' she rationalized between clenched teeth.

"No can do. We have to get this story in.''

"Then why did you offer to take me home to change if you had no intention of doing so?''

"I didn't. You came to that conclusion all by yourself.''

"But you said . . .''

"I said I thought you'd want to go home to change. I didn't say I'd take you.'' He stopped at the van and, unlocking the door, hopped in and reached across to release the passenger door.

Katie jogged lopsidedly around to the other side, grumbling, "I should have known better than to think he was turning into a human being.''

Hauling herself into the van, Katie buckled in and bent to assess the damage: one shoe, a brand new pair of pantyhose, and a skirt that was likely to give the cleaner fits. She should have been madder than a wet hen, but she wasn't. Instead, she was filled with a strange rush of excitement.

"I've never seen so many crazy people in one place.'' Katie made a futile attempt to finger-comb her hair as Lenn turned the van onto the freeway. "It was like a civil war out there.''

"Hardly,'' Lenn laughed. Sort of. Actually, it was closer to a snort. "The only similarity is that no one cared who got hurt. In a real civil war, they use guns and grenades, and innocent bystanders lose a hell of a lot more than the heel of a shoe.''

Katie twisted in her seat to stare at him. He wasn't just making a vague comparison. There was real anger in his voice and in the tightened muscles around his lips. "You sound like you've been in one."

"I was in Nicaragua for three years," he admitted with a quiet absence that indicated his thoughts were there now.

"What were *you* doing in Nicaragua?" Katie couldn't contain her surprise.

Lenn shrugged out of his reverie. "I guess you might say I was a war correspondent."

"*You* were a war correspondent?"

"Well, in a manner of speaking."

"When?"

"A couple of years ago."

"Why?"

"When? Why?" he parroted with a wry grin. "I knew you were still as nosy as you used to be."

"Never mind that. Tell me about Nicaragua. Who on earth sent you to such a dangerous place?" She was sure it hadn't been Sal. He'd hardly send his own son into a war-torn country, and besides, she'd have heard about it before now if that had been the case.

"No one *sent* me. A buddy of mine, Enrico Perez, was down there on special assignment. When he failed to make contact after three months, I started to worry and went after him."

"Couldn't the State Department have checked into it?"

"Yeah, sure," he derided. "They said their hands were tied. They couldn't interfere. They didn't have any influence down there."

"The usual runaround."

"Yeah. So I used my press credentials to get into

the country." Lenn looked over his left shoulder as he signaled a lane change.

"Did you find your friend?"

"Yeah." He inhaled a deep breath. "I trust you'll be wearing pants the next time I see you."

Katie raised a brow as she took in the studied calm that slid over Lenn's face. "Why'd you change the subject?"

"Because I'm bored with it."

"I don't believe you."

"Then maybe," he snarled, "I just don't want to talk about it anymore."

"All you had to do was say so."

"I'm saying it now."

"Fine," Katie snapped. Only it wasn't fine. Her head was buzzing with questions. She thought she knew Lenn so well, but he must have seen and done a lot in the years he'd been away. Had his experiences changed him as much as Sal and her father insisted? She shot him a discreet glance. It appeared as if every ounce of his attention was focused on steering the van off the freeway and into the *Newsprobe* parking lot, but she was sure his mind was elsewhere. She wanted to know exactly where. And why.

Lenn pulled into a space, switched off the ignition and leapt from the van, all without uttering a word. Katie stiffly climbed out and followed him, irritated at the silent treatment but not knowing how to break it. He didn't speak until the elevator opened at the newsroom floor.

"When you get that film developed, just leave the prints in the darkroom. I'll pick them up." He stepped out of the elevator. "That'll give you time to run home and change."

Katie looked askance at him. Was he actually being nice? She watched him lope down the corridor. Nah, he couldn't be. He just didn't want to be seen with her looking this way.

After Katie finished developing the shots she'd taken, she slinked down the fire exit in her stocking feet, feeling a little like a bad guy in one of the Nancy Drew books she'd read as a kid. Darting furtively between the rows of cars, she prayed no one would see the mess she was in. When she came to a sleek low-slung yellow Corvette, she stopped. Reverently, she slid a loving palm along the shiny fender and sighed—then she got into the battered red clunker slumping next to it. With one last lingering glance at the dream car in the next space, she sputtered out of the parking lot.

A short while later, she let herself into her apartment, flung her crippled shoes into the bowels of the hall closet and collapsed onto her deep futon sofa. She stared resolutely at the ceiling. Working with Lenn, she decided, wasn't as bad as she'd anticipated—it was worse. She wondered how someone could change so much and yet not change at all. With a disgusted sigh, she reached a hand behind her head and fumbled absently around the end table until she located her cigarettes and lighter. Savoring a long satisfying drag, she vowed, as she had for the past six months, that she would quit the disgusting habit *tomorrow*.

Lenn. A vision of his unwelcome face shimmered in the stream of blue-gray smoke she exhaled, causing her to pull on her cigarette with such vigor that the whole inside of her mouth burned.

Katie swung her feet to the floor and stabbed her cigarette into the ashtray. Thudding down the carpeted hallway to her bedroom, she slammed to a halt when she caught sight of the horror reflected in the dresser mirror.

She looked even worse than she felt. Her shoulder-length copper hair, naturally kinky to begin with, was matted into a bird's nest. She half expected a flock of sparrows to flap out of the tangle when she touched it. Her lips were starting to swell from the slap she had taken, and her chin was scraped raw. How that had happened, she couldn't imagine. And her brand-new skirt was spotted with dark runny splotches. Coke. She smelled like a bottle of Coke.

She had a good mind to call her father and get him over here to see the mess his plotting had caused this time. He and Sal. Butch and the Kid. She still hadn't figured out what they were up to when they talked her into taking this job. But they *were* up to something. She was sure of that. They were *always* up to something.

After showering and nursing her wounds, Katie made a bologna and mayo sandwich, which she ate in the car on her way back to the newsroom. The entire fifteen minutes the trip took were spent thinking about Lenn—again. She remembered the unfathomable look on his face when he'd refused to talk about Nicaragua. There had to be a reason for that reticence, and she was beginning to think that the reason went pretty deep. Maybe deep enough to account for the change Sal kept insisting his son had undergone. His actions this morning hadn't indicated much change. He was still as unpredictable and as goading as ever, but for that one moment in the van, when he talked about his friend, there had been something more. Something that was pulling at her.

She couldn't think of one single reason why she should want to know what made Lenn tick, but she did. He hadn't liked it when she'd tried to probe, but he'd get over that. And when he did, she'd try again. She couldn't help being curious. Okay, she conceded. Nosy. But sooner or later she was going to get him to tell her all about it. Preferably sooner.

Lenn felt someone staring at him. Raising his head, he glanced around to satisfy himself that everyone was as hard at work as he was. He shrugged off the feeling and returned to the keyboard. But it didn't go away, that odd discomfort of being observed. He looked around again, and this time his attention was drawn magnetically to the swinging doors.

Katie. The sight of her poised at the open door wrenched at his gut. No, make that a target considerably lower. He bypassed her face and let his gaze travel down the length of her well-shaped body, which was now encased in a pair of very tight jeans. The short skirt she'd worn earlier had showcased a lot, but it hadn't revealed quite as much as that well-worn denim. Now *there* was a body a man could hold on to. He wondered how a gawky, chicken-legged carrot-top had blossomed into someone as sexy as the woman standing in the doorway. He smiled—actually he leered, and he knew it—and shifted his inspection to her face. A face that could be classified as ordinary if it weren't for her lucid sea-green eyes. Those sea-green eyes were the one thing about her that hadn't changed, and he thanked the good Lord that some things in life stayed the same. Lately he'd been starving for a little familiarity, a little predictability, a little *sameness* to chase away the haunts. Katie, despite all the outward changes, somehow represented that familiarity.

Watching her cross the room, he knew she was still thinking over what he had let slip in the van. He hadn't meant to tell her about Nicaragua. He didn't want to tell anybody. And Katie, being Katie, wasn't about to let it lie. He knew that. Years ago he had used her insatiable curiosity as a source of amusement. He would make up wild tales that went on and on before she'd finally catch on that he was pulling her leg. She used to go off in a sulk. If he tried the same thing now, she'd probably threaten to beat him to a pulp. Hell, she'd probably do it, too. All five foot nothing of her. He'd have to be damned careful from now on. Nicaragua wasn't the kind of thing he could make up a story about to distract her. It was too real, too painful. He would never block out the sordid memories of bloodshed caused by a war he perceived as totally unnecessary. He could never forget Enrico or— No! God help him, he did not want to think. Not now. But he would never forget. Nor would he ever talk about that time. Not to anyone.

He could tell by the way she fidgeted with the collection of pens and pencils in his Mickey Mouse mug that she was trying to figure out a way to pump him for information. Just as he was trying to figure out a way to divert her from that intention. If it were any other subject, he'd sit back and enjoy the game. But the stakes were too high. This was one time he *had* to win.

THREE

Katie twirled a felt highlighter between her fingers.
She was aching to drill him about Nicaragua. There
were a dozen or more questions tripping about on
her tongue, but when she opened her mouth to voice
one, all that came out was a lingering, "So . . . ?"

Lenn leaned an elbow beside his keyboard and
propped his chin on his fist. He made no effort to
meet her eyes like a normal human being. He merely
stared straight ahead—at her chest. "So what?"

Katie could feel her nipples strain against the soft
knit of her cherry-red T-shirt. Damn him. He was
doing it on purpose. Giving the pen an extra hard
spin, she resisted the urge to cross her arms in front
of her. She wouldn't give him the satisfaction. If he
thought she was going to be put off by a leer or two,
he had another think coming.

"Um . . . I'm curious . . ."

"Yeah? And what else is new?"

She ignored the dig. It took a considerable effort.

44

"Yeah. I'm interested in finding out a bit more about Nicaragua. I've never known anyone who's been in that kind of situation. I'd really like to know what it was like."

"Then why don't you read up on it? It's been in all the papers."

"I don't read newspapers. Don't like 'em. That blasted ink gets all over your fingers."

"You don't read papers!" Lenn gaped at her over the monitor. "And you're gonna work for one?"

"Yeah, well, that's why I figure I should know a little more about what's going on in places like that. I mean, if I'm going to be dealing with current events and all. Don't you think?" Katie was proud of the subtle tack she had taken. She hadn't asked about the things she really wanted to know. Like what had happened after Lenn found his friend? And why he'd stayed so long, and how he'd gotten out? Or any of the good stuff. And it hadn't been easy because, normally, there wasn't a subtle bone in her curious body. Certainly not where Lenn was concerned.

"Damn it." He reached up and stilled her hand. "Will you stop knocking those pens around. You're getting on my nerves."

Katie jerked her hand away from his, dropping the pen back into the cup with a clatter. "Sorry."

"It's okay. Just go sit down some place, will you?"

She nodded and sat on the corner of his desk.

"So, how come you don't want to talk about it? If I remember correctly, the thing you loved most in the world was talking about yourself. Here's your chance." She flashed him a smile for good measure.

"I can't right now. I've got to get this story finished.'' Lenn turned to the monitor, deliberately tuning her out.

She waited for a moment. ''When *can* we talk about it?''

''Some other time.''

''When?''

He sighed, glancing up at her. ''When I feel like talking, I'll let you know, all right?''

''You're just saying that to shut me up.''

''Bingo. Now be quiet so I can work. And, uh, as nice as that backside of yours is, I really can't concentrate with it parked on my desk. So would you kindly remove it?''

Katie stood up, uncertain whether to feel flattered or rejected. ''Are you afraid to talk about it? I'll bet you are, aren't you?'' She shoved her hands into the back pockets of her jeans and shifted a toe to play with a gum wrapper someone had dropped on the floor. ''Well, fears are normal. Everyone has them. Take me, I'm afraid of flying, but they say if you talk about what bothers you, it sometimes helps—''

Lenn stood with a jerk and slammed his palm on the desk, causing everything on it to rattle and everyone in the room to stop what they were doing and stare their way. He lowered his voice to hiss at her. ''Mind your own damned business, Katie. I've had it with your questions.''

Katie's heart lurched, pounding so fiercely she could hear it drumming between her ears. Whatever else Lenn Domina was, she'd never known him to be so ill-tempered, or to react so strongly about *anything*. Obviously, she had nicked a sensitive nerve with her questions, and it finally dawned on her that more had gone on in Nicaragua than a search for a friend. Aching with regret for having been so ruthlessly curious, she backed off slowly, her eyes locked with his. In the depths of those angry flashing eyes, she could see scars that no amount of conscious effort on his part could conceal, and she felt a stirring of empathy for what he had endured.

Her palms were sweating, she realized, and she wiped them against the rough denim as she pulled her hands from her pockets. "I'll go down and get the photos and take them in to Sal," she murmured. "Let me know if anything breaks."

Lenn slumped back into his chair. His burning rage fizzled so abruptly she could almost hear it. He nodded, answering quietly, "Okay."

"Okay," she whispered and walked away.

"Katie?"

She glanced back at him. "Yes?"

Lenn hesitated for a long moment, then shook his head. "Nothing. I'll meet you in Sal's office."

The afternoon took a long time passing. After Sal approved the pictures and story, Katie and Lenn took one of the paper's vans and went looking for another newsworthy incident, without success. The traffic was heavy, the smog thick, and the atmosphere crackled with emotional energy. Neither of them spoke. It was as if a mutual pledge of silence had been made. At five o'clock they gave up their search and returned to the office. They checked in and out with Sal, then shared the elevator down to the main level of the building and walked out to the parking lot in polite, strained togetherness. The irritation she felt when Lenn continued in the same direction as she was headed turned into outright surprise when she discovered that the coveted Corvette slinking in the spot next to her car belonged to Lenn. She was dying to comment, but not wanting to be the first to break the silence, she held her tongue.

The weather was still sticky hot, and they were both reluctant to slide into vehicles that were simmering pockets of accumulated heat. Lenn crossed his arms and leaned against his car, watching Katie dig for her keys. He felt like a heel for the way he'd jumped down her throat earlier. Her curiosity was part and parcel of who she was. Hell, her perseverance was even something he actually admired. He'd known she was going to dig; he should have been able to maintain control. But he hadn't. As a result, he realized he would have to handle the matter differently than he'd planned. "I'll make you a deal, Red."

She didn't look up. "What deal?"

"Have a beer with me and I'll tell you about Nicaragua." He intended to keep it general—tell her about the country and a little about the war. Just enough to get her off his back, but not anything that really mattered. It was the only solution he could see if he wanted to keep his sanity.

She warily averted her attention away from the jumbled contents of her purse. "Really?"

"Really," he grinned. She looked like a puppy that had been given a lifetime supply of rubber bones.

"Are you serious?"

He nodded.

"Your car or mine?"

"Mine."

"Can I drive?"

It was a plaintive plea if he'd ever heard one. Lenn laughed outright. "If you want to."

Katie's mouth practically watered. "I want to."

He reached into his pocket and tossed her the keys. She caught them with a jubilant smile, then jogged merrily around the sleek vehicle and slid into the driver's seat.

"The physical danger was only part of the problem for a reporter trying to cover what was happening down there," Lenn explained as he dusted salt into his mug of beer. "What was really daunting was trying to get the facts straight."

Katie leaned on the dusky-rose tablecloth with her chin perched on her palm. "Why was that?"

"Well, Central America, much like Vietnam to some extent, was—and is, I guess—a contest for public opinion." Lenn took a long swallow of beer and licked a dollop of foam from the corner of his mouth. Katie felt a shiver that had little to do with what he was saying. "Sometimes it seemed as if ideals, or even politics, didn't really matter to either side. What was important was how the public, or actually the U.S. government, perceived the issues rather than the true issues themselves. It came down to money and how to convince people and governments to part with it. Because, you see, money can buy more guns and grenades." He leaned back in his chair and sucked in a heavy sigh. "Ah hell, maybe I saw it that way because I can't see the sense in any war."

Katie didn't say anything as Lenn finished his beer in silence. For once, questions weren't popping onto her tongue. Oh, they still swam inside her head, but for some weird reason she found she couldn't ask them. Maybe when she got home she'd take her temperature. She had to be sick.

"Look, Katie," Lenn finally spoke again. "I know you want to know more, but could we just leave it? The whole bloody mess makes me angry."

"Okay." Katie couldn't believe she was so willing to concede. For once in her life, she was going leave her curiosity unsatisfied. She tried to tell herself she was holding back because she didn't want to spark off another outburst like the one earlier. She tried to tell herself she didn't care to know that much about Lenn anyway. She hated him, didn't she? Why should it matter what had happened to him in the past? What she didn't try to tell herself was that she was a liar.

A golden-blond waitress, wearing a dainty pink dress and wide smile, approached their table to clear away their platters of half-eaten burgers and fries. Lenn greeted her with a grin of easy familiarity. It was obvious he'd been there before, and Katie wondered how well he knew her. The woman seemed to have a penchant for touching his shoulder while she spoke. Katie pretended not to listen to their breezy banter and deliberately let her gaze wander around the trendy little lounge.

The part of her that wasn't eavesdropping saw a dim, nostalgic kind of room, with walls covered with dated posters of Joni Mitchell, the Beatles, and other heroes of the same era. Music from the late sixties and early seventies played softly in the background, mingling with the tinkling of the wind chimes that hung in the open, stained-glass windows. Each time a stronger breeze passed through the room, the Spanish curtains would join in with a gentle chatter. A large brass ceiling fan hung low, its draft flirting with the edges of the rose napkins folded prettily on empty tables.

Lenn ordered a couple more beers, and the waitress finally left, leaving behind the lingering flowery scent of her perfume. For some reason Katie couldn't explain, she would have preferred it if the woman smelled like a funeral parlor. After she brought their second round of drinks and *swung* herself back to the bar, Katie turned to Lenn.

"So, do you come here often?"

Lenn glanced at the waitress bending over to take an order from another table and raised a knowing eyebrow. "Often enough."

"With anyone special?"

Lenn grinned. His damned white teeth actually glinted. "I'm flattered you're interested in the competition."

"When pigs fly. I was just trying to make conversation." Katie cursed her runaway tongue. Well, at least she knew she wasn't sick. Her curiosity was back in full force. That *was* the only reason she'd asked.

"Sure."

"Oh, shut up, Lenn."

"Are we going to start fighting again?" he asked. She could swear his voice was flavored with amusement. "I wouldn't give you the satisfaction."

"Too bad. I rather enjoy our little tiffs. Gets the old heart pumping."

"If you start needling me, I'm going to leave."

"Go ahead." He nodded toward the door.

Who was she kidding? She looked toward the window and stayed put. Dusk had fallen. There was no way she was going to walk down Sunset Boulevard after dark. Suicidal, she wasn't. And since her first paycheck was still a speck on the horizon, she couldn't afford a cab. So instead of leaving, she swallowed her pride along with a mouthful of beer. "Maybe I'll wait for you."

"I kinda figured you would."

"Stop laughing at me."

"I'm not laughing at you, I'm enjoying you. Is *that* okay?"

"I . . . I suppose." In spite of herself, her insides warmed at the off-beat compliment; nevertheless, she gave him a quizzical glance. Was a dash of playfulness sneaking up between them, or was she imagining it? And why did she like the idea?

Lenn continued smiling for a moment before letting the amusement fade from his face. "I guess I should apologize for biting your head off earlier."

"You should," she agreed with a suspicious look. Lenn Domina apologizing? "Aw no, I guess you shouldn't. I kind of had it coming."

"Not really."

"No, I know when I've stepped over the line, and I did."

"No, you were just being you."

"Well, even *I* know when to say when—" Katie stopped in midsentence when Lenn began laughing softly. "What's so funny?"

"We are. We can't avoid an argument, even when we're trying to be nice to each other."

Katie made an effort not to smile, or worse, laugh with him. He was, after all, the enemy. "I wasn't trying to be nice to you," she denied, pulling a pack of cigarettes out of her bag.

"Yes, you were. Look, there's a hint of a smile twitching on your lips."

"There is not."

"Is too. Oh, come on," he teased, reaching over to tug at the corner of her mouth with a thumb. "Give in to it. It'll feel good. Trust me."

Trust him, hah! She'd as soon trust that snake he'd stuck in her sleeping bag all those years ago. Pulling back from his touch, she tucked a cigarette between her lips, then coughed on the smoke when he screwed his face into an expression that was meant to mirror her own intentionally serious look. She had to laugh then. And it did feel good. Darn him.

After that, a strange thing began to happen. Well, strange for her and Lenn, at least. The laughter evolved into a lighthearted conversation, which in turn evolved into a moderately serious discussion of human psychology, of all things. By the time he pulled into the lot at *Newsprobe* so she could pick up her car, she realized that she had exposed more of her feelings to him than she would have liked. Not that she had any great secrets, but a few minor ones might turn into egg on her face if he ever decided to use them against her. And past experience made her suspect he would. Doubt began creeping up on her as he stilled the engine.

Lenn swung his arm onto the headrest of her seat, and began to toy with a wayward curl at her shoulder. "You know, the evening doesn't have to end yet. You could follow me to my apartment. We could listen to some music, sip a little—"

"You must be out of your mind." Katie jerked

her hair out of his reach and made a grab for the door handle. "Just because we managed an hour or so of civil conversation, don't take it to mean anything more."

Lenn caught her arm. "Why not? You've got to admit the chemistry's right."

"You're out of your mind. We've been at each other's throats ever since you found out I was your photographer this morning." She tried to free herself from his grasp, but she only succeeded in making him pull her tighter—and closer. And in spite of her denial, she responded to the nearness of him, the smell of him.

"That's exactly what I'm talking about. The sparks that zing between us. Think what could happen if that energy was properly channeled." Lenn nuzzled her sensitive earlobe, sending a shiver over skin already raised with goose bumps.

"You want sparks?" she breathed, pushing him away. "Go stick your finger in a light socket, and leave *me* alone." She heaved the door open and jumped out of the car. For once, the first grab into her purse came up with her keys, but she could hear his laughter, low and resonant, behind her as she fumbled with the lock and clambered into her car. She even heard it as her car chugged out of the lot and onto the street.

Two blocks down, she turned a corner and pulled to the curb. Every nerve in her body throbbed, especially those in the pit of her stomach. The closest she could come to naming the feeling inside her was *fear*. Yet it wasn't exactly that, either. Lenn might have changed, but he was still as intense as he had been as a teenager. Only now that intensity had a different direction. A direction that disturbed her even more than it had then. She never would have believed it possible, but he stirred a response in her that she did not want to feel. A response she knew better than to feel.

She knew he was the kind of man who would make a pass at any female who was breathing. From what her brother told her, she was certain that the old "chemistry" angle was a standard in Lenn's bag of tricks. Chris had been pretty tight with his boyhood chum since he'd been back in town, and he'd kept her informed about Lenn's prowess with the ladies. Chris, no slouch in the female department himself, bowed at the altar of his cohort's exploits. In her brother's mind, Lenn was a man to be emulated. Katie, being a woman, hadn't been quite so impressed. The tales of his sexual adventures made her dislike him even more, if that was possible.

Then why wasn't she able to raise that hatred now? She had pretended disgust at the time, but that hadn't been the case. For an instant, one unguarded moment, she'd been tempted to call his bluff. To find out exactly what he had been offering. Because the chemistry he had used as a line was real for her. Sometime during the evening, she'd stopped viewing Lenn as the obnoxious, self-centered boy she remembered from her childhood and had started to see him as a man. A man who wanted her in spite of their differences. She just had to keep in mind that she was only one of many. The last thing she wanted was to become a feather in Lenn Domina's cap.

With a long, calming sigh, Katie started her car and pulled back into traffic. She would try, for Sal's sake, to get along with Lenn, but only for a week. One week—if they couldn't learn to get along like two normal, mature adults within one week—she was out of there.

FOUR

Katie paced back and forth in front of Lenn's desk. Where was he? She'd arrived fifteen minutes ago, at nine on the button, and it had been an effort. Punctuality wasn't exactly her strong suit, but this morning, it was Lenn who was late. She felt like a fool trying to look nonchalant as she leaned casually against his desk, but for some inexplicable reason, she didn't want to sit in *his* chair.

The darkroom was being used, and apparently photographers weren't assigned desks like exalted reporters. She'd have to talk to Sal about that. She felt silly milling about. If she had a desk, she could at least pretend she was working. On what, she didn't know, but she could sure learn to fake something.

"Here, check this out." A rolled-up copy of the paper slapped into her hand. Reflex made her close her fingers around it as she gave a startled jump.

It figured. He'd sneaked up behind her when she wasn't looking. Typical. And she was beginning to think he'd changed. Hah! She whapped the paper back at him, landing it against his taut stomach. "I told you, I don't read papers."

"But our story's on the front page. Don't you want to take a look?" He flipped open the paper and shoved it in front of her.

She ignored it. "Look, I don't want to play Ping-Pong with that paper, and why should I want to look? I know what happened. I was there, remember?"

"Uh oh, a little cranky this morning, huh? You should have taken me up on my offer last night. You'd be a heck of a lot more mellow this morning." Lenn waggled his eyebrows. Katie was torn between laughter at the bad Groucho Marx imitation and anger at his audaciousness. He flipped the paper onto his desk. "Coffee's just the thing for a morning grouch. I'll spring for a cup. Anything happening around town yet?"

"I haven't a clue. *You're* the reporter." Katie gave an exasperated sigh as Lenn sauntered over to the coffee maker and filled a couple of Styrofoam cups. This getting-along business sure was trying.

The minute Lenn's back was turned, she stole a quick look at the full-color picture spread across the front page of *Newsprobe*. *Her* work. An unexpected rush of pride enveloped her. To think that the entire city would be holding that very paper in their hands. Feasting their eyes on *her* photograph.

Out of the corner of her eye, she saw Lenn pick up the cups and begin to turn around. She leaned a casual arm on the top of his monitor, facing away from the paper as if she'd merely been waiting for his return. Lenn stopped a couple of times to exchange a greeting with his fellow reporters as he wove a path between their desks, and Katie couldn't help but notice how well he filled out that faded pair of jeans. If they were any tighter, they'd have to be surgically removed.

He handed her the cup of steaming coffee. The hot, strong smell wafted under her nose. She took a needed swig as she watched Lenn swing a spare chair from behind an empty desk, then shove it wordlessly next to his desk before settling his lean-muscled behind onto his own. So he had a great body. So what.

Katie flopped onto the chair and sipped her coffee. Lenn carefully clipped and filed his story before turning to the crossword. She made a mental note to start a file of her own—when Lenn wasn't looking, that was.

"Well, how's it going with Danny boy?" he inquired without raising his head.

"How did you find out about Daniel?" She was certain she hadn't mentioned the name of the man she'd been seeing regularly.

"Hey, us reporters have our sources. What's a six-letter word for—?"

"You've been checking up on me?" she sputtered. Chris. She'd have to put a muzzle on that brother of hers. A tight one.

"I told you I like to know the competition—although he doesn't sound like he's going to give me much of a run. What are you doing with a fossilized old dinosaur like that anyway?"

"It's none of your business." She knew Dan was a few years older than she was, but he wasn't exactly carrying a cane yet. "I don't poke into *your* love life."

"Maybe you should. You might learn something."

"Might catch something, too."

"Uh uh, I'm *reeeal* careful about that." Lenn grinned knowingly over the paper.

Well, she *had* started it, but suddenly the conversation was getting a little too open for her tastes. Katie could feel a heat creeping along her skin. A change of subject was definitely in order. "So, what are we going to do all day? Sit here gawking at each other?"

"Who's gawking? *I'm* keeping my mind occupied." He rattled the paper and filled in another word.

"What mind?"

Lenn sighed in exasperation, dropping his pencil, eraser first, onto his desk. "What is it with you? I thought we'd met each other halfway last night. But today you come in here with both pistols blazing. Why?"

Katie couldn't answer. She bent over and pulled her camera and a lens cloth from the bag she had set beside his desk earlier. He was right. She was being, she knew, nothing short of nasty, and for once, Lenn hadn't really given her cause. Well, other than goading her about Dan.

With studied care, she wiped the lens of her camera, then raised it to her eye to check for nonexistent dust. Lenn stared at her though the aperture. He looked hurt, almost. Unreasonably, her heart missed a beat.

Finally he said, "You know, I'll bet I know what your problem is."

Defensive, Katie reverted to the sarcasm she had fully intended to quash. "I can't wait to hear it."

"It's that boring old patriarch you've saddled

yourself with. You're getting old before your time." Lenn rocked his chair onto its back legs and locked his hands behind his head. "What do you do for fun? Read the obituaries?"

"Yeah, I keep hoping I'll find your name." Katie's guilt had evaporated the minute he got back on her case about Dan. If the truth were known, she might agree that her relationship with Dan was not as exciting as she would like, but she wasn't about to give Lenn the satisfaction of knowing that. "Daniel is an intelligent, mature man. I like being with him."

"Maybe I'm missing something here. What about passion?"

"What about it?"

"You're even worse off than I thought. What a waste."

Katie tried to concentrate on cleaning her lenses, but she could feel his hot gaze on her. He was trying to make her aware of her body, of her passion. And he was succeeding. She looked up to glare at him. It was a mistake.

Her eyes locked with his in a sizzling battle of wills. She wanted to look away, needed to, but couldn't. It was as if there was a deep eddy swirling in the dark-brown depths of his eyes, a whirlpool pulling her helplessly deeper.

Lenn was the one who broke the contact, thudding his chair back on all fours. "Let's get out of here. There's got to be a story out there somewhere. Let's find it."

Katie recovered her sanity with a jerk. "Good idea. I can't wait to get out of here." She slid the lens she'd been polishing back into its felt-lined pocket.

Just then, Sal poked his head out his office door. "Hey, Lenn, get your tail over to Hawthorne. An apartment complex on Jefferson is on fire."

This time Katie was prepared and kept pace with Lenn as he sprinted into action, and if she managed more efficiently because she had worn jeans this morning, she didn't admit it to either Lenn or herself.

When they arrived at the scene, flames were darting high into the air from every window and a large section of the roof of the older wooden structure. The heat was beyond anything Katie could ever imagine, and the devastation wrought on the families huddled in small frightened groups made pictures that Katie captured with heart-wrenching sympathy. The firemen fought a losing war, battling rampant, wind-fueled flames that, by afternoon, engulfed the entire block. Confusion abounded, and no two people told the same story as to how the fire had started. Aching for their losses, Katie followed Lenn as he interviewed family after family. And when a fireman was injured, they followed the rescue van to the hospital and got his story as well, returning to the scene as the blaze was finally dying and control was in sight for the exhausted crews, who had fought valiantly the entire day.

Not until nine o'clock that evening were Katie and Lenn able to talk to the Fire Department spokesman, who was able to tell them the cause of the fire. In the lingering twilight, Katie sadly snapped a shot of the blackened, gaping void that once had been filled with apartments and homes, the occupants long gone, taken in by friends or family or by caring organizations. She heard the tired, smoke-roughened voice of the fireman tell Lenn that the fire had started when a Mrs. Gonzales, from suite 205 of the Rand Apartments, poured hot bacon grease into a garbage can on the back balcony of the second floor. Apparently, someone else had dropped some kerosene-soaked rags into the bin earlier, and the instant the grease hit them, they had ignited. The old wooden balcony was engulfed in minutes. Mrs. Gonzales had escaped by leaping from the balcony and had been taken from the scene before Lenn and Katie arrived. She was in the hospital with a broken leg and multiple burns.

After a futile trip to the hospital—Mrs. Gonzales wasn't seeing anyone, let alone the press—they returned to the *Newsprobe* building. Their dragging footsteps echoed in the empty halls as they separated to do their respective jobs. Lenn didn't have to tell Katie that they couldn't go home to rest, or to change smoke-imbued clothes, until the story was in and the photos processed. This time she knew her pictures could bring offers of help for those families left homeless, and she was as anxious as Lenn to see the job done. She sighed as she slid the last print into the dryer. Maybe, just maybe, she was on her way to becoming a news photographer. What she had seen had twisted her insides, and at times, she had felt a little ghoulish for snapping pictures of other people's misery. But if her photos could prevent one person from acting carelessly as Mrs. Gonzales had, or spur one person to cough up a little help for those affected by the fire, then it was worth it. She was tired and hungry and smelled like a chimney, but she felt darn good.

Lenn was hunched in the empty newsroom, clattering away at the keyboard. The sleeves of his red-checkered shirt were rolled to his elbows, exposing golden-brown forearms that were powerful beneath a semitransparent mesh of dark-brown hair. Her gaze traveled up and across broad shoulders, settling for a moment on the glossy dark hair that curled just above his collar. The inspection took seconds, but the strange flutter it caused in her stomach lingered long minutes. She meandered over to the coffeepot. It was, needless to say, empty. She laid her photos on the counter and scooped a pungent measure of granules from the large red tin into a filter and set it into the machine. Filling a jug at the water cooler, she complied with the laminated instructions taped to the wall. She stared unseeing at the machine as it gurgled, trickling fresh coffee into the carafe. Every pore of her body was aware of Lenn's presence in the large vacant office. It was as if the heat of his body pervaded the room just as surely as the hot, strong smell of the coffee assaulted her nostrils. It was a strangely discomforting feeling. She put it down to the eeriness of the deserted building.

When the coffee was ready, she filled two cups and carried them over to Lenn's desk. "Tired?"

"Yeah. You?" He took the offered cup as she nodded. "Thanks."

"How's it going?" she asked, leaning against the desk next to Lenn's and sipping the coffee she held in both hands.

He'd already gone back to work. Taking a swallow from the cup in his left hand, he tapped at the keys with his right. "Just about done. One more paragraph, and I'm out of here. How'd the pictures turn out?'' he asked without raising his eyes from the monitor.

"Good. I think. They're over there." She nodded toward the counter with the coffee machine. "I'll get them in a minute. I don't feel like moving right now."

Lenn gave a nod of understanding and leaned back to scan what he had written as he pressed the key to scroll.

"Do you do this often?" she asked.

"Do what?"

"Work this late to get a story in."

"Enough." Lenn tapped in a correction.

"Do you enjoy it?"

"What?"

"Do you like this lifestyle, working till all hours, rushing about . . . you know?"

"Yeah, I like it. Wouldn't do it if I didn't. Now, can you quit yattering? I'm trying to concentrate."

"Fine," Katie snapped, and Lenn felt a twinge of conscience. Well, she *was* bothering him, though it wasn't with her questions. It was those damned tight jeans so close to his line of sight. How the hell could he pay attention to the words on the screen when what he really wanted to do was run a hand over the sweet curve of her bottom? If her muscles were as tired as his, it would do them both good.

Damn. He'd run another couple of words together. Why didn't she just give him the pictures and go home? He tapped angrily at the keys. Katie pushed away from the desk and moved toward the counter as if she'd read his mind. He tried not to, but he watched as she moved across the room with easy grace. Damn, that behind of hers was an eleven and then some. He was going to have to do something about the attraction he felt for her. And soon. Before he went nuts with frustration. Every incredible little wiggle she managed to put into her walk was driving him crazy. If he wasn't so deep-down tired, he'd give another shot at trying to talk her into going back to his apartment, but as it was, he wished she'd move that delightful rear out of here and leave him to his job. Lenn sighed, dragged his eyes back to the monitor, and tapped out the last few words that finished his story.

He flipped on the printer just as Katie returned with the stack of photos. Wordlessly, he held out his hand, and Katie slapped the pictures into it with a little more force than necessary. Boy, she could hold onto irritation longer than any woman he knew.

"Hey, these are great. The night editor's going to have a tough time choosing which ones to run."

"Well, don't sound so surprised."

"I'm not. You know, we make a pretty good team."

"Professionally speaking, yes."

Lenn couldn't stop the grin. "Professionally speaking." And personally speaking, if had his way. And he intended to, but for tonight he was going to bide his time. A low chuckle vibrated through his chest. "We're quite the pair, though. A studio photographer who doesn't read newspapers and a reporter who doesn't know which end of the camera to look through."

Katie had to smile with him. His grin was infectious and he knew it, the conceited oaf. "You've got a point."

"Only you think it's on the top of my head, right?"

"Well, Domina, you always were pretty astute."

Lenn threw back his dark head and roared. How could she stay mad at someone who laughed when she scored a shot?

He ripped the copy out of the printer and clicked the machine off. "Let's blow this pop stand. It's nearly two-fifteen." He glanced at his watch as he tossed the story and photos onto the night editor's desk. "We've done our share for today." Lenn threw an arm over her shoulder, and although Katie told herself she should draw away, she didn't. They walked down the corridor in comfortable silence. The eeriness Katie had felt earlier in the empty building was unaccountably gone, and when Lenn removed his arm to press the elevator button, she felt strangely bereft.

Katie slid behind the wheel of her car, a shiver of goose bumps creeping up her arms in the cool morning air. Lenn leaned into the open window after he shut her door, and out of nowhere, tossed her a question. "How come we haven't seen each other over these past few years? I've been in town now and then, and I saw the rest of your family on the odd occasion, but there was no sign of you."

"Because," she answered levelly, "I've gone out of my way to avoid you every time you were in town."

"Why?"

"How can you ask that after the hell you put me through?"

Lenn stared over her car into the darkness. "Yeah, I guess I was a little tough on you back then."

"Back then?"

"You mean you think I still am?" Lenn glared into the car with an air of injured offense that was betrayed by the tiny glint in his eyes.

"Sometimes." *Why am I smiling?* she wondered, noticing that she was. *I'm supposed to dislike this guy, and here I am smiling idiotically at him at two in the morning.*

"You can be pretty tough yourself—*sometimes*."

"Yeah, well, you bring out the worst in me."

"Don't apologize. It's been kind of enjoyable, in an odd sort of way."

"Is that why you're still leaning on my car at this hour?"

"Could be." His mouth quirked at a distinctively mischievous angle. "Could damn well be."

"You're warped, you know."

"So I've been told."

Katie stifled a yawn. "I hate to spoil your fun, but I'm bushed. Do you think you could let me out of here?"

Lenn gave an exaggerated sigh and pushed away from her car. "You did good work today. I was impressed with the way you handled yourself."

Katie angled him a suspicious glance. A compliment? From Lenn? Especially one that sounded sincere. "Thanks." She shrugged a narrow shoulder. "That's what Sal's paying me for."

Lenn looped his thumbs in his pockets and rocked back on his heels. "Money well spent. Well, see you in the morning. Or in a few hours, I should say. *Ciao*."

"*Ciao*," she echoed as she backed out of her space and turned out of the lot, her face still scrunched in a puzzled expression that deepened when she glanced into her rearview mirror. Lenn was still standing by his car as if he would have liked to chat a while longer. It crossed her mind that she wanted to do the same, even though only moments earlier she had been dog-tired. She couldn't understand it, and she didn't try.

After a quick shower to wash the smoke out of her hair, she crawled into her bed. As wiped out as she was, she still had to agree that, professionally, she and Lenn did make a great team. Now if he would only stop looking at her as if she were naked.

Daniel called her before she left for work Friday morning, wanting to know where she'd been all week. She told him she'd taken up with a band of Hare Krishnas and had sought solace in the Mojave Desert to cleanse her soul. Miffed, he hung up on her. *Tough*. After nearly a year, she figured he should know better than to nag at her before she had her first coffee.

So, it was Friday. The last day of the one-week trial period she had promised herself. Monday had been a nightmare, Tuesday hadn't been too bad, Wednesday and Thursday had been iffy. Today would make it or break it.

It was also payday. Darned good thing, because all she had left in her fridge was a bowl of macaroni salad, three bruised apples, and half a bottle of flat Coke—and a tin of tuna for Rocky, the neighbor's cat. She wondered how much money she'd take home after Uncle Sam took his cut, then she swallowed a slug of dead Coke, gagged, and left the apartment.

_____ FIVE _____

Lenn was already at his desk when Katie arrived munching on one of the jelly doughnuts she had bought in the cafeteria at the *Newsprobe* Building. His long legs were stretched out to the side as he slouched in his chair, reading a hard-cover book and wearing, of all things, a pair of white pleated pants. This from the man who harped at her for dressing up too much for work. Darn, why did he have to look so good?

Katie skirted his feet and laid her camera bag on the desk she had finally managed to cajole out of Sal. Lenn glanced up, and his eyes lit up like two pen flashlights. "Hey, a jelly doughnut. Can I have a bite?" He hastily slid his book under a newspaper and stood up.

"Are you kidding?" she sniped playfully—yes, playfully. "I'd rather kiss a dog on the lips than eat after you. Here." She tossed the bag containing a second doughnut on his desk, trying to look as if she was making a supreme sacrifice when she'd actually bought the extra treat especially for him.

Lenn grinned a thanks without the slightest hint of remorse. "Want a coffee?"

"Yeah. Please," she tacked on with a yawn as she folded down onto her chair. She stole a watery glance around the room. Of the twelve other desks scattered around the office, three were manned by equally tired-looking reporters hammering away at their VDT's and chugging coffee to stay awake. She and Lenn had worked late again last night, and she was beginning to realize that losing sleep was an occupational hazard. She supposed she should be making an effort to acquaint herself with her co-workers, but the thought was fleeting. Why bother? She was only there until Sal found a replacement, right?

She flicked a quick glance at Lenn. His back was to her as he got the coffee. Furtively, she stole a peek at the book he had tucked under the paper. *Poetry! Lenn?* Dropping the paper as if it were on fire, she quickly made herself look busy before Lenn turned around. *Elizabeth Barrett Browning?*

Lenn strolled back and handed her the coffee. "Hey, did you hear that the good Samaritans of our fair city set up a fund for the victims of that fire? Sort of makes you feel proud that a story we did got that kind of response, doesn't it?"

"Yeah, it does." Katie closed her eyes and took a heavenly sip. "Mmm, I needed that."

"Yeah, I've noticed. Why do you think I go out of my way to get you a cup every morning?"

Katie's eyes popped open, pushing her eyebrows up into a questioning glare. Lenn grinned. "It's pretty obvious you're one of those people who isn't worth a pinch until she's had her morning jolt of caffeine.''

Katie wished she could argue the point. She also wished Lenn hadn't pegged her so easily.

"So," he flopped into his chair, "how's your old man these days?"

"Oh, Dan's ticked off because I haven't been home every time he's called this week."

Lenn sputtered into his coffee. "Ah . . . I was talking about your father."

Katie could feel her face turning into a beet. She wished the floor would open and swallow her and her fuzzy brain into oblivion. "He's fine. Uh, just fine."

"Glad to hear it." Lenn was having a hard time holding back a full-blown laugh.

She hoped he choked on it. "I know what you're thinking, and I don't want to hear it!"

He raised an innocent brow. "I didn't say *boo.*"

"Keep it that way."

Lenn pulled the doughnut out of the bag and sunk his teeth through to the jelly. "What have you got planned for the weekend?"

"I don't plan that far ahead." Katie hid behind the rim of her cup.

"Yeah," he said, his tongue darting out to catch a glob of jelly before it landed on his chin. "I suppose it must be pretty hard to make plans when the old dinosaur could croak at any given moment."

"Can it, Lenn. I don't need it this morning." She didn't yell—oh, she wanted to, but she didn't. She spoke calmly and evenly, quite pleased with the way she was managing to hold onto her composure.

"What you do need is pretty obvious."

"Uh uh, it's not going to work. I'm not going to let you get under my skin today. I'm onto your game. You're just trying to get a rise out of me."

"Wanna bet?"

"What do you mean?" she asked cautiously.

"Just that. I'll bet before the day is out I'll get under your skin, but good."

Katie met the challenge in his eyes with her own. "Not a chance. As I said, I know your game."

"Enough to shake on it?"

"What are the stakes?" Her eyes took on a brilliant gleam.

"If I win, we have dinner. A real date," he clarified to make sure she didn't miss the point.

"And if *I* win?"

"I'll stop teasing you for good."

"Hallelujah. You're on," she grinned naughtily, stretching her arm across her desk to slip her hand into his waiting one.

"Lenn!" Sal barked as he flung open his office door and lumbered over to their desks. When he spotted them holding hands across the desk, his voice mellowed discernibly. "I've got a story for you guys, if you want it."

Katie plucked her hand out of Lenn's. "What story?"

"You remember that principal at Valley View High School who imposed those dress codes that had all the kids picketing? Robert Bonaduce?"

Lenn nodded. "Yeah, what about him?"

"He just called. Claims he's been unfairly dealt with in the press. Everyone's interviewing the kids and twisting what he's been saying. Seems he's a

Newsprobe fan and thinks we'll give him a fair shake. He wants to tell us his side of the story. You want it?''

Katie answered for both of them, her insatiable curiosity piqued. ''Yes, we want it.'' She was dying to hear the story firsthand.

''Go for it, then.'' Sal flashed a self-gratified smile and sauntered back to his office, pausing at the door to look back. ''By the way, I'm glad to see you kids getting along better these days.''

Sal's words bounced around Katie's brain during the drive to Robert Bonaduce's home. Getting along better? Wherever did he get a fool idea like that? She and Lenn would get along about the same time Sonny and Cher got back together. She hazarded a peek in the enemy's direction. Even though his eyes were glued to the road, she could see the glint of mischief hidden in their depths. He was thinking about the bet. She could see the wheels turning and she shivered, suspicious that before the day was over, he'd be leaving tread marks on her back. So much for getting along. Boy, was Sal ever wrong on that one.

Almost as wrong as Lenn if he was thinking he was going to win that bet. She'd developed a fair amount of control since she was a kid. True, she had to admit she hadn't exactly exhibited much of that hard-learned ability since he'd slammed back into her life. But she could when she wanted to. And boy, she wanted to. The very idea of not having Lenn bug her for the rest of her life was sheer heaven. Not that he'd be around for the rest of her life. She planned on making sure of that, but for some weird reason, she couldn't help wondering what it would be like if he were. At least she'd never be bored. A man like Lenn would keep a woman on her toes just trying to stay out of the line of fire whenever he decided to be *playful*. Actually, that might not be altogether bad. Good Lord, where had that thought come from? *Get with it, Katie. Remember all those times Lenn acted like an out-and-out jerk. Remember all the things you've heard about his reputation with women. Remember last week when you damn near melted just because he nuzzled your neck. Remember what could have happened if you hadn't . . .*

Katie closed her eyes. No, she'd be better off not remembering *that* little incident. She'd thought about it all too often these last few days—trying to convince herself Lenn wasn't sincere about wanting her. But she always returned to one truth. For all Lenn was, and for all the character flaws he had, he was at least honest. Even with all the pranks he had played and all the teasing he had done, she couldn't ever remember having caught him in a lie. Not even a little white one. Not even to spare someone's feelings, and especially not hers. In fact, there were times when she actually caught glimpses of kindness flickering in the depths of his eyes. What a bloody complex man.

And what a bloody ridiculous turn her thoughts had taken. Who cared what made Lenn Domina tick? And why on earth was she even thinking about him? She must be out of her mind.

"What's on your mind?"

Is there an echo in here? She shook her head and gazed at him blankly. "What?"

"I asked what was on your mind. You're awfully quiet. That's not like you."

"Oh, did I finally do something right in your humble opinion?"

"Hey, you do things right by me all the time. You're sitting right by me now. You walked right by me on your way to your desk this morning."

Katie tried to stop the smile, but it sneaked out despite her efforts. "Oh, Lenn, be quiet."

The corners of his mouth lifted in obvious satisfaction. "Okay, but only if you'll tell me what had you so deep in thought."

"Oh, sure. Do I have *sucker* stamped across my forehead? The minute I start talking, you'll make fun of what I have to say. I know you."

"Maybe too well," he muttered, adding, "But I'm really not that bad. Am I?"

"Yes, you are."

"Oh, come on. The other night at the cafe—we talked. I didn't *make fun* of you then."

"Yeah, well . . ." She hesitated, not knowing whether to trust her instincts. Where *was* he headed with this conversation? "I guess you were reasonably easy to talk to then," she admitted.

"Reasonably? I think I rated a little better than that."

"Yeah, well that always was your problem."

"Huh?" He took his eyes off the road for a second to furl his forehead in her direction.

"You always did figure you rated a little better than the average Joe."

"Well, don't I?"

Katie threw her arms up in surrender, then shifted her gaze resolutely out the window.

"So," he persisted, "what were you thinking about?"

Bahk! I give up! "Life, okay? I was thinking about life and relationships and . . . I was just drifting."

"You getting bored with Old Dan?"

Well, now that you mention it . . . No, idiot. He'd have a field day with that one. She lied through her teeth. "No."

He cast her one of his high-voltage you're-lying-to-me glances and stated with quiet conviction, "Yes, you are. And the sooner you admit it, the sooner you'll stop wasting your time and let yourself develop a real relationship."

"Oh, sure," she chuckled. "With you, I suppose?"

"Hell, no. The last time I tried th— Uh, I'm not into relationships. At least, not the kind that require actual work. But I could make you happy for a little while." He flashed a half-serious, deliberately lecherous grin. "Very, very happy."

She knew exactly what kind of *happiness* he was promising, and the prospect of setting herself up to be used wasn't high on her list of priorities. "Thanks, but no thanks."

Lenn stared thoughtfully at the road for a little while. "Remember that dirt bike my uncle Luciano bought me when I was fifteen?"

"Yeah. What an old bucket of bolts that was." She glanced at him quizzically. "Why do you ask?"

"Do you recall your reaction the first time I offered to take you for a spin?"

"Sure. I was astonished. It was the first time you ever offered to do anything nice for me."

"It was not," Lenn insisted, a little-boy look of hurt on his face. "But that's not what I'm trying to get at. You refused, remember?"

"Well, of course I did. First of all, you weren't

old enough to be on that stupid thing, and secondly, you didn't need an accomplice to dig potholes in people's lawns. You were doing just fine on your own.''

"Will you never mind all that?" he snarled in exasperation. "I'm trying to make a point here."

"Oh, pardon me—sir."

Lenn rolled his eyes toward the roof of the van and sighed. "Anyway, eventually you did go for a ride with me, and you loved it."

"Yeah, when I wasn't worried about you throwing me off every time you took a corner at top speed." She shook her head at the memory, at the excitement she didn't want to admit she had felt back then. "But what's the point you're trying so hard to make?"

"My *point* is this; now you're saying no, you absolutely don't want what I'm offering. But I know you well enough to know that deep inside you're attracted to the unknown, to adventure, and sooner or later you'll give in."

"Hah!"

"And what's more, you'll love it—just as much as you loved the bike ride."

"God, you're conceited."

"I wasn't talking about *that*. I was talking about the thrill of doing something because you want to, because you get a little tingle just thinking about it."

"Hey, Romeo, I've got a little newsflash for the hotshot reporter. I don't get a little tingle at the thought of hopping into your bed. I get the creeps."

"Damn it, Katie, that's not what I'm trying to get at."

"No?" She looked him doubtfully, then started to laugh. "For a guy who boasts of having more women than he knows what to do with, you sure seem to be desperate for a little body heat.''

"Aw, man,'' he groaned, ''don't you ever let up? I'm trying to have a serious conversation here, and you think I'm working an angle.''

"You are. You're trying to bait me into losing it so you can win that bet we made,'' she said with absolute certainty. ''But it's not going to work.''

Lenn snorted. "I've already got that in the bag. I just thought it might be nice to talk. To get to know each other better. I didn't plan for the conversation to turn out the way it did.'' *At least not this time*, Lenn added to himself. Oh, he did intend to make her lose that volatile temper of hers, but he had most of the day to do that. He really had wanted to talk, and he was surprised at how much it bothered him that she'd misread his motives. Well, if he was going to be hung for the crime, he might as well have the pleasure of committing it. He glanced out the back window to make sure the lane was clear and swung the van onto the off ramp.

"Sure, Lenn. And if I were to say, forget the bet, I'll go out with you anyway, what would you say?''

There went that little tingle he'd challenged her with, only it was in his own gut. ''I'd say it was about time. I'd say name the hour and the place, and I'll be there. That what you're saying?''

"Not on your life.'' She offered him a mischievous grin which he couldn't help but return.

"You really can be a little . . . witch when you want to, you know.''

"I know,'' she replied, unoffended. ''That's what makes me so adorable.''

Lenn felt his jaw drop. She'd shaken him for a

minute there—she'd sounded just like him. And damned if she didn't have a point. Her saucy streak appealed to him more every day.

He slowed the van as he turned onto the street where Bonaduce lived. There was a small shopping complex on the corner of the block of neat, middle-income homes. Number 342 was the third house in from the mall. Pulling the van to a stop, he hitched his canvas bag under his arm, swung out the door and started up the walk, expecting Katie to follow him. When he didn't hear the usual scurrying slap of her sneakers behind him, he turned to see her wriggling off in the wrong direction.

"Hey, it's this way." He gestured over his shoulder at the tidy bungalow.

"I have to make a call." Indicating the phone booth on the corner, she continued in the direction she was heading. "Go on ahead. I'll join you in a couple minutes."

"Why can't you use Bonaduce's phone?"

"Because . . ." she paused to glance back, "it's a personal call."

"Oh." She was probably going to phone Danny-boy. How personal could a conversation with a creaky old business suit get anyway?

Shifting his weight from one foot to the other, he watched her enter the phone booth, deposit a coin, dial, and lean against the dusty glass. He supposed he should mind his own business and get started on that interview. Sure. As soon as the sun turned green.

Katie stood with her back to him on purpose, he didn't doubt, so he couldn't read her lips—not that he knew how. He couldn't see her expression, either.

Well, he thought, starting toward the phone booth, there was only one way to find out what she was saying. When he realized he was treading on tiptoe like some back-alley cat burglar, he forced his gait into a casual stroll. He could tell her he didn't want to cause awkwardness by having to go through the introductions to Bonaduce twice. Yeah, that sounded good. He was only waiting for her and he didn't want to do it standing in the middle of the street. *Domina, you're being an obnoxious S.O.B. and you know it.* But, hey, all's fair in love and war. Not that *love* had anything to do with it.

Leaning against the exterior of the booth, he listened shamelessly, though it didn't do him any good. Dan was apparently doing all the talking and Katie all the listening except for an occasional, "Uh huh . . . uh huh . . . uh huh."

Really, he thought sarcastically, *if those two didn't cool it down, they'd be shorting out the wires.* But then he overheard her saying, purring actually, "All right, Daniel. I'll see you tomorrow. Around noon?"

Not if he could help it! For one tiny second, he considered that what he was about to do was dirty pool. But only for an extremely infinitesimal second. If she jumped down his throat, he could remind her of the bet. Perfect out. He squeezed into the booth beside her, grinned at her astonished face, then whispered into the phone, "Hurry, baby. The bed's waiting."

Katie tried to whack him with the receiver, but he was long gone. Fumbling with the phone, she managed to get it back to her ear. "Daniel—it's not what you think. Daniel . . . Daniel?" With a growl, she hammered the receiver back into its cradle and leaped onto the sidewalk like Superman in the cartoons.

Lenn stood about six feet away, his hands set cockily on his hips, his face beaming with an *I won* expression. Katie jerked up short. The desire to kill literally made her see red, and that was exactly what he wanted. That ridiculous bet. He'd done it to win that stupid, idiotic bet. It took every ounce of control she possessed, and then some, but she settled for grinding her teeth, thinking that if she spent much more time around Lenn Domina, she was going to be stuck with a whopping dental bill. She gulped back a couple of supposedly calming breaths and sauntered, as casually as her angry feet would allow, past the grinning ape. "It won't work. Daniel's a very understanding man. When I explain your *childish* behavior, he'll—" Her words were cut short.

Lenn grabbed her by the arm, whirling her around to yank her hard against his body. His mouth ground against hers, his tongue driving between her lips, forcing them apart. Katie froze, too shocked to react or to push him away. She felt an insidious rush of goose bumps shooting across her skin in rhythmic waves. His kiss softened, but it was no less demanding—demanding submission? And she, damn her traitorous body, was giving it to him.

Good Lord, how could this be? How could Lenn draw such a response from her when Dan couldn't even inspire a tiny tingle? In fact, that was why she'd lost interest in any kind of intimacy with him long ago. She couldn't make any sense of the way she was feeling.

Lenn slowly, reluctantly, eased Katie away. His hands slid down her back and closed around the intriguing curve of her hips. At this moment, she wasn't good old Katie anymore. She was a woman he wanted to make love to so badly his teeth ached. Hell, lately that was all he could think about.

The anger he'd felt when she'd taunted him about Dan had evaporated in the hot, sweet recesses of her mouth. He murmured into her hair, "See what happens when we touch? Why do you keep fighting what we could have?"

"Because," she breathed, her sanity finally returning, "contrary to what you believe, Lenn, it takes more than physical attraction to make a woman happy." She hadn't been raised to pass her body around as if it were a sample of some cleaning product to be used, then discarded.

She remained motionless while he slid his hands over her hips, forcing her mind to go blank so her body couldn't respond any more than it already had. With more difficulty than she would have liked, she cleared her throat and spoke firmly, and surprisingly calmly. "Don't we have an interview to get to?"

He released her abruptly. "Right. Save it for good old Dan." Turning with a grind of his heel, he added caustically under his breath, "For all the good it'll do you."

Katie sprinted to catch up, biting back, "If I didn't know better, I'd say you were jealous."

"Dream on," he snorted, stepping up to the door and leaning hard on the doorbell. *Jealous. Crud.* Jealousy was for insecure little boys who were foolish enough to let themselves get bent out of shape over some dizzy broad who . . . His thought died when the door eased open and a short, studious-looking character gazed expectantly up at him.

This was the hard-line principal who was standing up against some four hundred picketing teenagers? Lenn rolled his eyes heavenward. Someone up there was playing a joke on him, right? Why hadn't he refused this damned interview? It really wasn't his kind of story. Why? Because Katie had jumped on it, and he, in some stupid moment of weakness, hadn't wanted to disappoint her. Now he was stuck trying to worm a story out of Casper Milquetoast here. It was turning out to be one of *those* days.

Well, he might as well get on with it. "I'm Lenn Domina. This," he gestured with a jerk of his head, "is Katie O'Brien. We're here to get your side of the story."

Robert Bonaduce scratched the top of his head where the sun reflected off a balding spot, then stepped back from the door. "Oh, you must be from *Newsprobe.*"

"Obviously," Lenn grunted, making a quick surveillance of the modest, contemporary home. He spotted the living room to the right and marched toward it without waiting for an invitation.

Katie exchanged a shrug with the bewildered principal as they followed Lenn. Bonaduce perched his decidedly frail body on the edge of the only chair in the small living room. Katie glanced around and, seeing no other choice, joined Lenn on the sofa. He was yanking his recorder out of his pack, and Katie could see he was in a let's-get-this-over-with mood. Probably because he hadn't been able to goad her into losing the bet. Too bad. But he didn't have to take it out on poor Robert over there. Well, she knew there wasn't much *anyone* could say or do to persuade him to loosen the goldfish bowl he usually screwed tightly over his head when he got peeved. Certainly not her. But she could do her best to make it a little easier for the anxious little man they needed to interview.

Lenn plunked his recorder onto the coffee table. "Go ahead."

"Well . . . um . . ." Bonaduce began nervously. Katie was having a hard time reconciling this edgy, fidgeting man with the kind of person who would stand up to an entire school of teenagers. He had to be reacting the way he was because he was feeling the weight of Lenn's impatience pressing on him. "I . . . uh, don't really know where to begin. Should you not be asking questions or something? You know, to help me relax."

Katie shot Lenn a nasty glare before turning a smile toward the nervous principal. "Mr. Bonaduce, why don't you begin at the beginning?" Okay, so it was a rather worn icebreaker, but it still worked every time. "Tell us why you decided to impose this dress code on the students at Valley View High."

"Well, you see, it's a matter of principle. I believe that if the students take pride in how they look, they'll take pride in their work." Bonaduce leaned forward, almost eager to answer Katie's simple, straightforward question.

Damn her, now she was horning in on *his* interview. She was supposed to be setting up her camera and taking pictures—not asking the questions. That was his job. He was about to inform her of that little fact when he heard Bonaduce finally stop his annoying little *uhs* and *ahs* and respond to Katie's gentle probes.

It made him feel like a worm. He'd been taking

his frustration out on that poor, unsuspecting soul, when the person he really wanted to verbally crucify was the red-haired witch beside him. Katie, with her streak of curiosity that was as wide as the Grand Canyon, was firing question after question at the timid man. Bonaduce probably didn't know what had hit him. Lenn knew the feeling. And damned if she wasn't getting a good, detailed story out of a previously reluctant man. Well, he and his slightly bruised ego might as well sit back and leave her to it.

That resolve lasted all of five minutes. He wasn't used to letting someone else do the work, and he was getting bored. His mind began to wander. To scheme. To think about the bet. If he wanted to win, he had better get a move on it. Maybe he should start with something small and work his way up.

"So," Katie said, wondering what Lenn was up to when he dug into the bottom of his bag and pulled out a notepad and pencil; he *never* took notes. He usually worked directly from the recorder. She shrugged and returned her concentration to Bonaduce. "You say that only a few rabble-rousing teens are objecting to your rules? I understood that the entire student body has been picketing the school."

"Well, you see," Robert Bonaduce explained, "I'm sure—in fact, I know, that most of the students are being goaded into what they're . . ."

Katie's eyes were drawn to Lenn's notepad, despite her resolution to ignore him and continue with the interview she felt she was pulling off pretty well, considering that it was the first she'd ever tried. The rest of what Bonaduce was saying went right past her head. The words Lenn had been noisily scratching read, *Your place or mine?*

Resisting the urge to kick him, she returned her attention to the subject they'd come to interview. Lenn shifted slightly so that he appeared to be leaning forward, listening intently to the gentleman relating his story. He perched one elbow on his knee, and let his other arm fall loosely behind her back. She wished the sofa wasn't so short, and that Lenn wasn't so close, and that she couldn't feel his thigh burning into hers. But at least he'd snapped out of his coma and was joining the interview *he* was supposed to be leading in the first place.

She nearly jumped out of her skin when she felt his hand slip under the back of her T-shirt and creep up her spine. She turned her head to pierce him with a killing glare, but his eyes were focused on Robert Bonaduce, his face as innocent as an angel's. Anything she might try to do to stop him would draw attention to herself and her predicament. And *that* was an embarrassment she didn't need.

Discreetly, she moved a few inches away. Lenn, equally discreetly, followed. She moved again. He followed again, repeatedly, until she found herself pinned against the end of sofa. She was certain Bonaduce thought they were both nuts. Well, she fumed, at least he was half right.

In a desperate attempt to distract Bonaduce from their odd behavior, she fired another question at the puzzled man who was still perched nervously on his chair. Lenn's teasing fingers drifted slowly sideways. She was at the point of saying embarrassment be damned. He was dangerously close to her most ticklish spot when he suddenly withdrew, then leaned casually back to retrieve the notepad that had been abandoned on his jaunt across the couch. Her immense relief was short-lived when he began to scribble again. She was *not* going to look. No way. He could write until his fingers fell off. She was not going to look.

She looked. This time he had written, *Are you on the Pill?* and below that, *God, you've got a great a—*.

She had to get out of there. Fast. She jumped off the couch, grabbed her camera from her bag, and snapped such a swift shot of Bonaduce that he didn't have time to wipe the incredulous expression from his face. With a quick thank-you for the interview, she hustled out the door, leaving Lenn to scramble with his recorder and follow her.

The minute of fresh air she gulped in before Lenn caught up barely gave her the control she needed. Yelling would lose her the bet, but there wasn't any reason she couldn't hand him a verbal slap. "You do realize that you made us look like a pair of idiots in there." When that didn't put a dent in his cocky smirk, she aimed right for the jugular. "I thought you were a professional. I guess I was wrong."

She thought for a second that his eyes narrowed a tiny bit, but his grin held.

"You feel like going to McDonald's for a burger? I'm hungry?"

Hungry? He was hungry? "Do you know," she said with a sticky-sweet smile, "if you had a brain, you'd be dangerous."

Lenn scurried past Katie as she stalked to the van. He opened the passenger door, deliberately guiding her in a gentlemanly fashion. Knowing Katie, his show of thoughtfulness at this stage would add fuel to the fire he was certain was raging inside her. That he hadn't managed to ignite an explosion as yet was distinctly irritating. He had to get her angry enough to blow the irritating cool she was hanging onto. Somewhere along the line, the bet had taken on a different purpose. He wanted revenge—for everything from that jealousy crack, to the slam about his professionalism—and forcing her on a date, since she was so dead set against it, was the best way he could think of getting it. This was war. And as he drove the few blocks to a Golden Arches, he thought of the perfect ammunition. Good old staid, irritating Dan.

Katie stared down at the cheeseburger and fries Lenn plunked in front of her. He hadn't even asked what she wanted. Without a word, certainly not one of thanks, she got up and went to the counter, ordered Chicken McNuggets and a salad, paid for her purchase, and went back to the table. Lenn had tucked away the burger he'd ordered for himself and was calmly digging into the one he'd bought for her. It took some of the wind out of her sails. She hoped he gained ten pounds and split those damned sexy jeans of his.

She slid a furtive glance at the big clock on the back wall. It was just after one. She didn't think she'd be able to last the day. Eyeing the phone outside the ladies' room, she wondered if Sal would give her the rest of the afternoon off. It might be a coward's way out, but she could claim to be sick. It wouldn't be a lie. She *was* sick—sick of Lenn Domina.

"So, you figure old Dan will forgive and forget?"

For a minute Katie considered giving him the silent treatment, but decided he might misconstrue that as having gotten under her skin and claim he'd won the bet. "Yes, as a matter of fact, I do," she lied, figuring she could maintain at least some semblance of control for the short time it would take to eat. After all, she was kind of hungry, underneath the anger. But after that, she fully intended to call Sal.

Lenn stabbed a French fry into the puddle of ketchup he'd globbed onto the wrap from his burger, then threw her a look of pure disbelief. "You know, I'm having a hard time understanding this *relationship* you've got yourself bagged into. The man's old enough to be your father. From what I hear, all he's got going for him is money." He paused, his burger nearly at his mouth. "Or is that the attraction? I'd have never thought you were the type to prostitute yourself for a few bucks. If that's the case, I've saved a few bucks. Why not auction yourself off to the highest bidder?"

Before she realized what she was doing, her hand sliced through the air and connected with his cheek. The slap was loud enough to draw gasps from everyone looking on. And many were, since the place was packed. She didn't care. Lenn's eyes, once he recovered from the initial shock, glittered like black diamonds. She didn't care about that, either. Grabbing her bag, she stormed between the tables and left the restaurant, ignoring the tall, ferocious form following her.

He caught up to her at the edge of the parking lot, twirling her around with such a jerk she was sure she had whiplash. "Damn it, Katie . . ."

Katie yanked her arm free and indignantly tossed

her hair back. "You've said enough." She wasn't about to listen to another word from him, but she intended to get in a few of her own. "You know, last night I went to bed thinking that with a little effort, we might be close to getting along. I must have been out of my mind to have believed, even for a split second, that you might have changed. You *never* will."

She didn't give him a chance to answer. Spying an empty cab cruising by, she leapt off the curb and flagged down the surprised driver. L.A. wasn't exactly New York where that sort of thing might be common, but the man didn't blink an eye when she hurtled into the backseat and told him to step on it.

SIX

Because there wasn't a live person around to listen to her complaints, Katie spent the better part of the afternoon and evening fuming at her furniture. What really burned her was the idea that she had almost—almost—believed that there might actually be a sensitive, caring human being beneath all of Lenn's push and shove. She should have known the whole thing was an act.

She said as much to Rocky, the cat, when he dropped in for his usual late-night snack. He didn't offer one bit of sympathy; he merely blinked, then curled up on the windowsill with his tail coiled around his ear—presumably to block out her tirade. After that rejection she had a good, stiff drink and went to bed.

The phone woke her at eight in the morning, but she pulled the jack out of the wall and went back to bed until noon, and after nearly twelve hours of sleep, she felt a little more optimistic about life in general. Well, maybe optimistic was overstating it a bit. She felt a little less angry at Lenn.

Shortly after one, she drove out to her parents' home in Malibu, thinking that spending some time with her family might cheer her up. Then again, maybe not. She was halfway there when she remembered that she was still angry at her father for helping to talk her into working with Lenn in the first place. She intended to have a little chat with him about that.

Charlie was puttering in the front yard when she pulled into the driveway and parked her ancient red Gremlin behind his sleek black Camaro. Perhaps it was the lousy mood she was in, but she looked at her father's fancy new vehicle, thinking that everyone she knew had a nicer car than she did.

With a depressed sigh, she folded into her father's arms, burying her face in his neck. He smelled of Old Spice, and his round stomach pushed into hers. It was a comforting feeling. She guessed she could put off lighting into him until she got her fill of affection. Charlie stroked her back soothingly, which, for some reason, made her want to cry. She took a deep breath instead.

"What's wrong, sport?" he inquired, holding her at arm's length. "Life got you down?"

"Yeah." Actually, it was Lenn who had her down, but she wasn't ready to bring him up yet. "Is Chris coming this weekend?" She slipped her arm around her father's ample girth as they walked into the house.

"Yes. Well, he said he was, but you know Chris. If he gets a better offer . . ."

"Come on, Dad. He's not that bad."

"Yes, he is. But that's our boy."

Katie considered it her sisterly duty to change the subject. "Is Mom here?"

"She's out back fussing with her garden," he said, holding open the screen door. "Let's you and me sit down, and you can tell me what's bothering you."

As soon as Katie entered the front door, the familiar scent of fresh-cut flowers filled her senses. She loved this old house, with its glossy hardwood floors, floral wallpaper, and big bay windows that let the sun pour in throughout the day. Grandma and Grandpa O'Brien had built their home in Malibu in 1930, the year they emigrated from Ireland, long before Malibu became *the* place to live. Last year, when Grandpa died, Grandma insisted on moving into a retirement home because she "didn't want to be a burden." No one in the family felt that way, but try getting that through her stubborn Irish head.

Every room in the house seemed to mourn their absence at times. Times like Good Friday, when Grandma would insist that everyone wear black, and Easter Sunday when the aroma of bread baking in the oven would have everyone wandering into the kitchen for a whiff. And Christmas, when the children would open their gifts, and everyone would get really excited. Everyone except Grandpa, who remained a placid old soul no matter what went on around him.

Katie sat at the kitchen table, feeling loved and secure for the first time in a week, quietly observing her father as he gathered the makings for tea. Slowly her tension began to subside. A balmy ocean breeze circulating through the white-and-yellow kitchen cooled the film of perspiration along her brow. It felt wonderful to be home. Her suite in Hollywood was nice, but this, she thought, was *home*.

"Say, where's Thunder?" Katie had been braced for an enthusiastic, wet greeting from the family dog and felt deprived, somehow, that it hadn't happened.

"Crazy mutt got into a fight with a humongous Shepherd. He's at the vet's."

"I might have known. It's becoming a habit."

"Yeah. I think he's getting cranky in his old age." Charlie set the shiny copper kettle on the back burner and turned on the heat. "So, how's the new job coming along?"

"Lousy." Yeah, that about summed it up.

"Why? You don't like working for Sal?"

"Sal's fine. I adore that man. It's his abominable son I can't handle."

"Oh—him." Charlie had the decency to look slightly abashed.

"Yes. Him. As if you didn't know."

Her father shrugged and turned his attention back to the whistling kettle. She should have known the conversation would turn to Lenn sooner than she wanted. He was omnipresent lately. His face—sometimes casting one of his cool reptilian glares, sometimes smiling that impish grin, sometimes showing no emotion at all—kept popping into her head. What annoyed her was that she had no control over the apparition. It came and went as *it* pleased.

"Dad?" She had to ask. "You must have known things wouldn't work between Lenn and me. Why did you help talk me into this mess?"

"Darlin', do you really think I'd set you up in a no-win situation?" Charlie placed the mugs and teapot on the table, pausing to look her in the eye before returning for the milk and sugar.

She shrugged. "That's just it. I have to be honest with you. I don't know what to think."

Charlie sat at the table and reached for her hands to squeeze them reassuringly. "I wouldn't do that, lass. Whether you believe it or not, there's a good side to Lenn Domina, and I know you'll see it once you learn to put the past behind you."

"That's easier said than done, Dad."

"I don't doubt that for a minute." Charlie cocked his head wryly. "But I think that if you give it a little time, it'll work out."

She gazed at him skeptically. "I think you're dead wrong on this one. I've got a short fuse, and he's got an even shorter one. Throwing us together is like tossing a match into a keg of dynamite. There's bound to be an explosion."

"My dear, what you have is simply a case of bad chemistry. Uh, no, make that *strong* chemistry." He echoed the words Lenn had used, and Katie felt a shiver along her spine, remembering how Lenn had demonstrated his theory.

"Lenn has a strong personality. So do you. I remember when you were a wee bit of a girl, your mother and I would get you to do something by deliberately telling you to do the opposite. Lenn's the same, only in a different way. He's a complex man, and he wants to have his own way. That's where the friction comes in between you. You're not about to let him." Charlie took a long swig of tea. "You know, Sal and I talked about this before he offered you the job. He thought that if anyone could handle Lenn, it would be you."

"Why is it so important that *anyone* handle him at all? He's been doing just fine all these years. Better still—why does it have to be me?"

"Because you won't knuckle under."

"That's all well and good. But how do I stop myself from killing him?"

Charlie shook his head. "I can't tell you that. Well, I could, but you'd only do the opposite," he teased, trying to lighten the mood.

"Seriously, Dad, what would you do in my place?"

He took a moment to consider. "I'd give him a run for his money, that's what *I'd* do."

"How?"

"Hang in there, just to spite him. Take everything he says with a grain of salt. The best way to deal with Lenn is not to take him seriously. Laugh. Have a little fun at his expense."

"Do you really think that would work?" The idea had a lot of appeal. Turn Lenn's jokes back on him. Yeah, that did sound good.

"I know it would."

"Well, I might give it a shot." *But only because I hate giving up. And maybe,* a part of her had to admit, *because I'm beginning to like the job.* "It can't get any worse," she added aloud.

"Well, don't blame it *all* on him. You said yourself you've got a short fuse." Charlie topped his cup from the teapot, then raised the pot questioningly at Katie. She shook her head. "You know, actually, Lenn reminds me of our Chris in a good many ways. Maybe that's why I like the lad."

"Oh, please. Chris could never be that impossible." But inside her a little voice screamed, *Wrong-o.*

"Yes, he can. You're just too close to him to see it."

"Chris isn't a womanizer."

"Well, now, I think you'd get a different idea about that if you talked to a few of his old girlfriends."

"I don't care. Chris is nice enough to get away with it. Lenn isn't."

"Lenn isn't what?" Vanessa O'Brien queried as she breezed into the kitchen carrying a basket of freshly cut flowers and smiling serenely, as usual.

"Doesn't matter," Katie replied, knowing how taken her mother was with Lenn.

"If I were your age and still single, well . . ." Vanessa let the implication trail as she reached into the cupboard for a vase. "That Lenn's a charmer."

"He's a skirt chaser, Mom."

"But a charming one, dear. He's so like our Chris."

"Will you two stop saying that? Chris isn't half the . . ." Katie sputtered, "the playboy Lenn is. That man should be locked up."

"My, my," Vanessa teased. "Aren't we touchy today?"

Charlie shot his wife a cautioning glance and, ever the pacifier, changed the subject. "Say, I thought you had a date with Daniel today. Not that we're not glad to see you alone, mind you."

Katie shrugged indifferently. "I just didn't feel like seeing him today."

"Isn't it going well between you two?"

"Yes. No. Oh, I don't know, Dad. He's getting to be . . . well, a bore. He was fun for a while, but now . . ." Her voice faded into thought. What could she say about her relationship with Dan? It wasn't bad—but it wasn't good, either. It was just . . . there. In the beginning, she had been fascinated with his tales of wheeling and dealing, until she began to realize that money, material gain, and power were all he cared about. Lately, she wanted more. What exactly *more* was, she wasn't certain, but she knew Dan Caldwell didn't have it.

"Well, dear, all the more reason to take a good look at Lenn." When Vanessa got an idea in her head, she stuck with it. "He's good-looking, well built, tall . . ."

"And he's got about as much respect for women as a dog has for a bone," Katie threw in before her mother went on to the point of nausea.

"Now, Katie, you're still angry about those little pranks Lenn used to play when you were kids. Lenn's grown up. So have you. It's time you forgot the past. You're entirely too rigid. Loosen up a little."

Katie stared at her mother in disbelief. Here was a woman who was normally an excellent judge of character, and she was going gaga over a dark-eyed bandit with a slow smile. "I can't believe that you, of all people, can't see through that smooth Latin charm of his."

Vanessa smiled. "I admit, he's got an aura of mischief about him, but that's what makes him interesting. Your father had that quality when we first met." She reached across the table to touch her husband's hand. "He still does."

Tell me about it, Katie thought. Mischief and Charlie O'Brien went hand in glove, but it wasn't the same thing. Lenn went way beyond mischief, but her mother, for some reason, didn't see that.

She looked at the couple staring into each other's eyes. If her mother really believed that Lenn had the same qualities as her beloved husband, Katie knew it was pointless to try to convince her otherwise. She might as well give up.

"I'm going for a swim. You two obviously need to be left alone. Honestly, at your age!" Katie grinned and pushed from the table, feeling a wash of pleasure at her parents' devotion—and just a tiny twinge of envy.

It was a lovely California day, characteristically warm, but with a steady breeze blowing in from the ocean. Katie spread her towel on the white sand and stretched out on her tummy to get some sun. With her red hair and pale skin, she didn't tan very well, but with an icy Coke on one side, a bag of tortilla chips on the other, and her copy of *The Thornbirds* waiting to be reread for the seventh time, well, it didn't really matter. This was the life. She cranked her Walkman up a few decibels, licked her finger, and flipped to the page where Father Ralph and Meggie met for the first time. As far as she was concerned, that was where the *real* story began.

The only problem with these wonderful, passionate romance novels was that they reminded her of how boring her own love life was these days. She thought of Dan. Not because he reminded her of the dashing heroes she read about, but because he paled in comparison. Some of the novels she read lately were so steamy that the corners of the pages curled, and when she finished one, she was left to deal with a great big yearning that dwindled rapidly when she looked at Dan.

Forty-four-year-old Dan Caldwell. Some women appreciated older men, but Katie, after having sampled one for nearly a year, was coming to the conclusion that they weren't all they were cracked up to be. At least Dan wasn't. Something was missing. *Life* was missing, and Lenn was right—*passion* was missing. She wanted, no *needed*, a man who would haul her into his arms and kiss her until she saw stars, no matter how old-fashioned that sounded. She was sick and tired of paternal good-night kisses. She wanted *excitement*.

Katie was tending the barbecue in the backyard when she heard an engine rumble softly into the driveway. She knew without checking that the smooth-running motor was housed in an immaculate white '57 Chevy with lots of gleaming chrome. Confirmation came a few moments later when her tall, handsome brother, clad only in skimpy cut-offs and sneakers, wandered out the back door.

"I knew you were out here somewhere. I could smell burning meat."

She smiled indulgently. "Good afternoon to you, too. I was hoping you'd make one of your cameo appearances."

He scanned the length of her figure wrapped in a form-fitting white sundress. "You're looking good, as usual."

"So are you. You on a real visit or just dodging some lady in hot pursuit of your bod?"

Collapsing onto a lawn chair, he sighed, "Both. Where's Danny-boy today?"

"Not here."

"Obviously. Can't say I'm disappointed."

Here we go again, she thought. "We're not going to start on that already. You just got here."

Chris drew his lips into a line and stared out at the hazy horizon. "He's too old for you, Katie. I'll hound you until you smarten up."

Sheer habit made her leap to Dan's defense. "He's a decent, mature man."

"Mature. Yeah, I'll go along with that. Decent? At his age, he probably doesn't have the stamina to be anything else."

"Damn it, Chris. No man I've ever dated has been good enough as far as you're concerned. Admit it. Brian wasn't too old."

"No. He was too stupid."

"There." Katie aimed the barbecue fork in his direction. "I rest my case."

"It's my duty to look after you. You're my baby sister."

"I'm twenty-six years old, Chris."

"That's not too old to get hurt."

Katie laughed out loud. "By *Dan*? Please."

"What do you see in him, anyway—besides dollar signs."

Not him, too. "I don't care about his money, and you know it. He's there when I need him. That counts for something, you know."

"Not enough. He's a bore."

"All right, then," she snapped, her patience wearing thin. "You tell me what I should look for, and I'll run an ad in tomorrow's paper."

Pulling his pipe from his back pocket, he tamped

the briar bowl with sweet-smelling tobacco and flashed her a dimpled grin. "Someone like me."

"Hey, if I could find one, I'd snatch him up so fast, he wouldn't know what hit him." She never could hold onto irritation around Chris.

"There must be a reasonable facsimile out there—somewhere."

Katie was saved from having to respond to that blatant statement by the arrival of their parents. Vanessa slid a tray containing a large bowl of her special potato salad, a basket heaped with golden rolls, and four frosted mugs onto one end of the faded wooden picnic table. Charlie made quick work of filling the mugs from the six-pack of beer he had under his arm. He passed them around before he and Vanessa sat at the magnetic chess board that was set up at the other end of the table.

It was a tradition in the O'Brien household that Vanessa and Charlie settled their disputes at the chess board. Whether it was the dishes, the laundry, or the grocery shopping that needed to be done, when neither wanted the chore, the chess board settled the issue, and the loser did the work. Katie watched them as she had many times before, a soft smile on her lips as she wondered vaguely what the stakes were this time. She knew, though, that it didn't really matter. It was the challenge they both relished, and it showed in the mutual sparks in their eyes.

"I hate to break up the game before it begins, but the steaks are ready." She piled the sizzling slabs of meat onto a platter and carried them to the table.

"Great. I'm starved." Chris levered out of the lawn chair and folded himself under the picnic table. His fork was into the meat before Katie's hand had left the platter. She shot him a scathing glare. He didn't even have the grace to look guilty. "Hey, I'm a growing boy."

She was about to tell him his growing was all sideways these days when they heard the arrival of another car in the driveway. With a who-could-that-be shrug, Charlie hurried through the house to the front door.

He was beaming from ear to ear when he returned moments later. "Look who's here."

"Hey, Domina, you old dirtbag. Pull up and have a brew." Chris popped the tab off a beer, and Vanessa scurried to the kitchen for another mug.

Katie all but swallowed her tongue. Lenn sauntered down the steps, his muscled thighs encased in his standard issue, extra-tight blue jeans. A white cotton shirt covered his back but flapped open over a tanned expanse of chest etched with a black-haired "T" that slipped below his belt. She wished he had the decency to button up.

The moment Vanessa returned from the kitchen, he greeted her with his usual kiss on the hand and accepted the mug of beer from Charlie with profuse thanks. They were lapping it up—that old-world charm he oozed when it suited him. It turned Katie's stomach. "What are you doing here?"

Charlie and Vanessa's eyes widened at their daughter's abruptness, and even Chris shot her a puzzled glance. She didn't care. Lenn Domina was not going to spoil a day that was just beginning to soothe the frazzled state that *he* had gotten her into in the first place.

"Ah, I knew you had forgotten."

Forgotten. She hadn't forgotten one single thing,

including Lenn's outrageous behavior of the previous day. She'd tried, though.

"Our date. You remember—the agreement we made?" Lenn said pointedly as he turned his soulful dark eyes in Vanessa's direction, knowing where sympathy would lie. But a second later, when he met Katie's incredulous glare, those same eyes were shot with taunting amusement. "I knew you must have forgotten when you weren't at your apartment, but I figured you'd probably be here. So . . . here I am. You ready?"

"Ready, you've got to be out of your—"

Her protest was drowned out by Vanessa's excited, "Why, Katie, you never told us you had a date with Lenn."

And Charlie's pleased, "You and Lenn have a date?"

And Chris's shocked, "*You* agreed to a date with *Lenn*?"

Katie was about to answer them all with a resounding *No* when she suddenly remembered.

Lenn knew the second that Katie recalled the bet. She looked as if she was going to choke. He didn't dare let her get in another word. When he'd thought up this scheme, he expected to bluff it out in private, then apologize for having pushed her so hard the day before. He'd wanted to win the bet, but he hadn't wanted to hurt her, and he knew he had. Last night, he'd had every intention of dropping the whole damn thing, but with the dawn of morning, he began to think that forcing Katie to see him on a personal level might be the best way to settle things between them. Now he was committed to getting her to spend the evening with him, and he hoped he was right about her not wanting to make waves in front of her family. Because if he wasn't, he was going to have egg all over his big mug, and he didn't mean the one he was draining of beer.

Katie knew she was stuck. Both of her parents were looking at her as if she'd given them an all-expense-paid trip to the Bahamas. If she denied she had a date with Lenn, Vanessa would be disappointed, and Charlie would think she wasn't keeping to her agreement to try to get along with Lenn. But it was her own nagging honesty that was giving her the most trouble. She had shaken on that stupid bet, and she had lost. True, Lenn had used underhanded, downright dirty tactics to win, but he *had* won. Well, she'd give him his date, all right, but she'd make sure it was the most miserable evening he ever spent—because she knew it was going to be the worst she ever had to live through.

"But we were just about to have supper." It was a feeble attempt at best, but it was her last shot. She knew it wouldn't work, and it didn't.

"Oh, you go ahead with Lenn, dear." Vanessa was only too happy to offer a solution. "Chris will be glad to eat your steak. You know he's a bottomless pit."

Katie fully expected her brother to leap on her steak right then and there, and if she'd been less aware of Lenn practically breathing down her neck, she might have noticed that Chris didn't seem to share the enthusiasm of her parents. As it was, she was too busy trying to think up ways to make Lenn regret this date he was forcing on her.

"All right," Katie admitted defeat. "But I'll be

home early," she said to her folks, although the point was made for Lenn's benefit.

Lenn held his tongue until they were out the front door. "What do you mean you'll be home early?"

"I'm staying here for the weekend." Outwardly, Katie still radiated antagonism, but she secreted an inward smile at the thought of thwarting any plans Lenn might have for seduction—not that she would be susceptible anyway. But now, if he expected to stay on the good side of Charlie and Vanessa, he'd be forced to bring her home at what *they* would consider a respectable hour. Smile, heck, she was holding back an out-and-out belly laugh.

She sat on the edge of Lenn's sofa, glaring at three candy-apple-red vases decorated with striking black Mexican designs. An insight into the complex man who had placed them in his apartment, they stood in stark contrast against the soft gray pinstripe of the wallpaper. Katie, however, was in no mood to appreciate either the room or what it revealed about its tenant.

Cupboard doors slammed. Drawers creaked shut. Glasses clinked. Pots rattled. Katie seethed. She'd assumed that the dinner that had been the stake of the bet would be at a restaurant. Arriving at Lenn's apartment had done absolutely nothing to calm her temper. She heard soft footfalls coming nearer as he entered the living room, and she quickly cast her eyes downward to stare stubbornly at the carpet.

Lenn sat on the arm of the sofa and drilled the corkscrew into the bottle of champagne he'd gone out of his way to buy earlier in the afternoon. He glanced down at Katie. Her eyes deliberately avoiding him, she almost seemed to be meditating. Contemplating murder, most likely. He smiled and sat for a moment observing her features, appreciating the tawniness of her long, thick eyelashes that were so close to the color of real gold that they mesmerized. She might not be a classical beauty but something about her drew him, though at the moment, the stiff ramrod set of her body was a trifle off-putting. "Relax. This is supposed to be fun."

"Being forced to spend an evening in your company isn't exactly my idea of fun. Just get this gourmet Italian meal you claim you can make on the table. The sooner we eat, the sooner you can take me home."

Lenn heaved a long, impatient sigh. He had known this wasn't going to be easy, but, damn it, she was pushing it further than she needed to. Why couldn't she give him a chance? He was trying his best to keep it light. "Hey, instead of staring at the floor, why don't you try looking at me for a while. Open your mind. You might like what you see."

Katie raised her eyes and stared steadily into his. "You really are a conceited bastard, Domina."

She wasn't prepared for his reaction. Faster than a blink, he dropped to her side, his steely hands gripping her shoulders. The champagne bottle, with the corkscrew still sticking out the top, dropped onto the coffee table, bounced off, and rolled under the sofa. "Quit rubbing my nose in it, all right? I won't take that from anybody, not even you."

"Rubbing your nose . . . ? What are you talking about?"

He pushed her away disgustedly. "Don't play ignorant, Katie. It doesn't become you."

Dumbfounded, she stared at him. "I don't know what you're talking about—honest."

Lenn's tone was sarcastic, his eyes hard. "Isn't that why you delight in giving me a hard time? Because I'm a *bastard*? Isn't that why you look down on me? Why you won't give me the time of day?"

For a moment Katie couldn't speak. When she did, she chose her words carefully. "So help me, Lenn, I didn't know." She stared across the narrow space separating them. A dark lock of hair coiled down his forehead. It would be so easy to reach across and smooth the strand back in place, soothe the brow beneath it. She clenched her hand in her lap and asked softly, "Why don't you tell me about it?"

"So you can gloat?"

"I won't gloat. We may not get along, but I think you know me better than that."

Lenn sucked in a resigned sigh. "I suppose if I don't tell you, you'll only ask Chris or Charlie. I still find it hard to believe you're the only one who doesn't know."

"Well, I don't, so tell me."

He looked at her for a long, strained moment, his eyes dark with pain, before he finally gave in and told her what she was so anxious to know. "When my mother was a baby, she was promised to Sal. They did that back in those days. You know, arranged marriages while the kids were still in the cradle."

The concept seemed unbelievably archaic to Katie, but she merely nodded, anxious for him to continue.

"Anyway, when Sal was seven, his folks immigrated to America, but even though the two families were separated, they intended to honor the deal. It was expected that when my mother reached marriageable age, Sal's family would send for her. Only, when my mother turned sixteen, she was seduced by the neighborhood Don Juan and ended up pregnant. It was a big disgrace back then, and her family was going to put her in a convent until she had her baby . . . Well, to make a long story short, Sal heard about it and sent for her. The minute she got off the boat, he married her to save her family's good name and prevent a scandal. I was born a few months later. And that's it. In a nutshell.''

By this time, Katie had edged forward and was perched on the edge of the sofa. ''When did you find all this out?''

''Remember that summer I went to live with my grandmother in Italy?'' Lenn glanced across the sofa at her.

Katie nodded. How could she forget? That was, until she'd met him again last week, the last time she'd seen him.

''I found out a few months before that. I overheard some of my aunts talking at a family gathering. Well, I went a little wild. Sal and my mother didn't know what to do with me. I was acting like a real brat, so they sent me off to Italy. I guess they thought that if I saw the way things still were over there, I might understand a little better.''

''Did you?''

''Not then.'' Lenn reached under the sofa and retrieved the champagne, and with a vicious twist yanked out the cork. ''All I could see is that one minute I was part of a happy family, the next I was the *bastard*. I thought they didn't want me around.''

"Oh, Lenn!" A pang of sympathy tore through Katie's heart.

"Damn it." Lenn exploded off the couch and slammed the champagne bottle onto the table. "I don't want your pity. Let's get this bloody meal over with. It's what you wanted all along."

Katie bounced up after Lenn, grabbing him by the arm just as he was about to storm into the kitchen. "No, Lenn we're not going to leave it there. I don't pity you. I ache for the mixed-up boy you must have been back then, but I sure don't pity you. Because I know how much Sal loves you, and, damn it, you must realize that by now."

Lenn shook off her arm, but he didn't move away. The hard set of his jaw softened almost imperceptibly as a tiny edge of his pain eased. "Yeah, I know. And I . . . well, I may not have a drop of his blood running in my veins, but I love him, too. But that really doesn't change things, you know."

He left the room then, and she didn't try to stop him. Her mind spun with questions. Why hadn't she known? Why had no one told her? The families were as close as any could be. Until Maria had married and moved to Nebraska, Lenn's sister had been a pretty good friend. She felt almost—betrayed. It made her realize how much worse it must have been for Lenn when he found out.

She was still standing, staring vacantly at the unlit candles on the table in the dining nook when Lenn returned carrying two fluted glasses. The air in the room was charged with awkward silence as he filled them and offered her one.

Katie held the glass in her hand but didn't drink.

She knew the muscles in her throat wouldn't enable her to swallow. "I don't know what to say."

"For God's sake, don't say you're sorry. That's one worn-out cliché I can do without."

"It doesn't matter, you know."

"Doesn't it?" he asked bitterly.

"No, not to the people who care about you."

Lenn took a long swallow of champagne, staring at her over the rim of the glass. "And what about you?"

Katie could see pained vulnerability behind the dark shadow of doubt that clouded his eyes. He took the glass from her hand and set it, along with his, on the table, then hooked a finger under her chin.

"Does it matter to you?"

"No," she whispered, fully aware of the implication behind the question.

His lips met hers, softly, achingly. The kiss was so light, Katie almost thought she must be imagining it. Lenn drew back, his finger still holding her chin, as he studied each individual feature of her face. Then, suddenly, she was in his arms, and he was claiming her mouth with an urgency that made her tremble.

All her senses came alive in that one kiss. She became vibrantly aware of the scent of his skin, the taste of champagne on his lips, the feel of his strong, hard body pressed against hers. Her arms moved of their own volition, sliding beneath his open shirt, moving across the taut, warm muscles of his back.

Lenn slid his tongue between her teeth. God, she tasted so sweet. She felt so damned good; her soft hands caressing his back were driving him crazy. He wanted those hands to work their magic on every aching inch of his body. Never had he felt a need so strong, so deep. In another minute, he'd take her here, standing in the middle of the room. Lord, he had to get her into his bed before he exploded. Easing his mouth away from hers, he heard the soft sigh of objection and looked down at the pliant woman in his arms. Her eyes, darkened with passion, were the deep green of a stormy sea, not the spitting cat color he was used to. The recognition brought a cool rush of sanity to his brain. Katie, the Katie he knew, should be fighting, pushing him away, accusing him of all sorts of evil intentions. Instead, she gazed up at him with soft tenderness beneath the warm desire. Tender, soft-hearted Katie was in his arms because she felt sorry for the poor *bastard*. But as much as he wanted her, and right now it was with a throbbing painful need, he didn't want her pity. He wanted the Katie who fought him at every turn. Aw, hell!

"I think the spaghetti's burning." He had to get out of here fast before his libido overruled what little was left of his mind. Practically jogging into the kitchen, he leaned his arms on the counter and jammed his head against the upper cupboard door. It was going to take a while before the need for that woman eased. He wanted her. And he still intended to have her, but it wouldn't be because she felt sorry for him. Pulling in a long, deep breath, he grinned. Knowing Katie, her sympathy wouldn't last very long. And then, lady, look out.

The spaghetti's burning? Katie shook her head. The action did little to clear the need that was aching deep in her loins. He'd done it to her again. He'd kissed her silly, made her believe he wanted her, when all the time his mind was on the spaghetti cooking in the kitchen. He'd taken her to those stars she'd read so much about, then dropped her back to earth with a resounding thud—exactly the way he used to set her up for a fall when she was a kid.

Only she wasn't a kid anymore. Hurt and disappointment welled in her chest as she moved toward the kitchen hoping to find in Lenn's dark eyes an expression other than the gloat she fully expected. She'd only taken three halting steps before she froze in her tracks. Through the door she saw Lenn push away from the cupboard, his mouth twisted in that familiar, self-satisfied smirk he always wore when he'd put one over on her.

Her anger rose to a white-hot fury. More than anything she wanted to retaliate, but to do so would let him know how much he had gotten to her. Katie filled her lungs to capacity with a calming breath. Pride had seen her through a childhood with Lenn, and it would see her through now. She could barely think straight, but through the bitter anger she heard Charlie's advice echo in her head. *Don't take him seriously. Turn his jokes back on him.* Well, it was a little late for part of that advice. She *had* made the mistake of taking him seriously. But she wasn't about to do it again. She was going to take her father's advice if it killed her. Now all she had to do was figure out how she could turn Lenn's little *joke* around so that he was the victim, not she.

Her mind awhirl with possibilities, she forced herself to smile and take the few remaining steps into the kitchen. It might take a little plotting, but her moment would come.

Lenn looked up over the colander he shook, expertly draining the steaming noodles. His face was still plastered with the impish grin he'd perfected at her expense. It cost a great deal of self-discipline not to physically wipe it away.

He cleared his throat. "Ah . . . what just happened between us?"

Katie leaned a shoulder against the cool fridge door, striking a deliberately casual pose. "I think that's pretty obvious."

"Not to me." Lenn sobered as he set down the strainer. "Did you respond so feverishly because you wanted me?" he asked. "Or because my . . . story touched that little girl in you who knows what it's like to be an outcast?"

If Katie hadn't known better she might have fallen for the wary flicker in his eyes. Luckily, she knew better. She smiled coolly. Her moment of revenge had come sooner than she expected.

"Neither. I simply got carried away by my fantasies." She waited for the cocky leer she knew he would flash when he made the assumption that he was the one she was talking about, then added, "For a moment there, I thought you were Dan."

SEVEN

Lenn pulled into her parents' driveway and braked with a jerk. If looks could kill, she would have needed the lives of a cat to have survived the last hour. For a moment back there in Lenn's kitchen, she had thought he would explode on the spot, but instead, he had slapped the spaghetti into a bowl, stalked to the dining area and thwacked the food onto the table, all without a word. But, oh, those looks.

Katie refused to be intimidated. She'd eaten the surprisingly tasty meal with all the heartiness of the winner of a championship bout. Lenn all but inhaled his serving, then hustled her out of his apartment with the speed of a rocket blasting into space.

For the entire silent drive, she'd smugly reveled in her victory, but suddenly she needed to get away from Lenn. Now. She unclicked her belt and reached for the handle. But he was faster. He levered out of the car and was around to her side by the time she was able to pull herself out of the low-slung seat.

With an ominous thud, he closed the door. She tried to duck around him, but he was too close. He moved closer, his arms caging her against the side of the car.

"Lenn, I—" It was a futile plea. His mouth covered hers with heated desperation.

Katie tried to pull away, to twist her head. She really did. For about five seconds. His tongue insinuated itself between her lips, gentling, teasing, destroying her sanity. She tried to remember that she would be a fool if she were taken in again. He didn't want her. He was trying to get back at her. She had to remember that. Closing her eyes, she tried to shut out the driving force of him, tried to remember that he was only—

Her eyes shot open. Lenn had pressed his body hard against hers, his hips forcing hers to meet the cool yellow metal of the car. A man couldn't pretend that kind of reaction. Could he?

What the heck. She slid her arms around his back. He tasted so good, felt so good, that it didn't matter anymore. Who cared why he was kissing her with such debilitating expertise? She wanted it. Needed it. Needed his mouth on hers, needed to return the thrusting probes, needed to answer the heated grind of his hips. She groaned when he pulled back, and the cool evening air sliced between them.

"Now, tell me you were thinking about good *old* Dan." Lenn shoved away from the car—and her. He was back in the driver's seat, with the engine revving to life, before she had the sense to pry her limp body from the side of the car. And the way Lenn peeled out of there, she didn't think he'd have stopped even if she'd remained plastered to the side.

Katie stared at the rapidly diminishing glow of taillights until the Corvette turned the corner three blocks up the street. What was going on here? Was he playing games, or did he really want her? She threw her arms up in disgust. The only thing she was sure of at this point was that she was getting a headache trying to figure him out. She turned and slowly scuffed into the house.

Chris, Charlie, and Vanessa were at the dining-room table playing gin rummy. Vanessa, as usual, had the biggest pile of toothpicks. Katie slid into the seat opposite her father, propped her head on a fist, and stared vacantly at the painting over his shoulder.

Chris folded his cards. "What is it with you and Lenn?"

Good question, she thought. "Nothing. Nothing at all."

"Bull. I know Lenn better than that. What's got into you? Don't you have any more sense than to go out with Lenn Domina, of all people?"

"Chris," his mother admonished, "I thought Lenn was your friend. Why shouldn't Katie go out with him? He's a charming boy."

"Yeah, he's my friend. And a good one. But that doesn't mean I think he should be dating my sister. Hell, that *charming boy* has slept with half the women in L.A."

"Now, Chris," Charlie sighed, "if I believed that, then I'd have to assume you'd slept with the other half. You two are peas in a pod. Have been since you were kids. You know you were in on most of the pranks Lenn used to pull on Katie. Never could understand why she only blamed Lenn."

"Dad, that was a long time ago. It doesn't have

any bearing on now. We're not kids anymore. Katie could really get hurt here.''

"Hold it." Katie's neck was getting tired from swiveling to follow the conversation. She was sitting right there for Pete's sake. Didn't she have anything to say in the matter? "Nothing is going on between me and Lenn. Didn't you hear me? And who do you think you are, telling me who I should go out with?" she growled at her brother. "Not that I'm going out with Lenn. I'm working with him. Period!"

"Yeah? Then what was tonight?"

"Nothing, I told you," she hedged. "We made a bet. He owed me dinner. That's it." Well, it wasn't that far from the truth. "It was a one-time-only shot. Could we just forget it?"

"Katie—" Chris started.

"Chris," Charlie interrupted pointedly. "Katie said to forget it. Stop worrying about your sister's love life and look after your own. That should keep you plenty occupied."

Chris looked as if he wanted to say more, but one thing the O'Brien kids learned early was that you didn't push when Charlie was wearing *that* look. "Right." He made a show of fanning out his cards. "Whose turn is it anyway?"

Katie declined when asked to join in but remained at the table, half listening to the banter between her folks and Chris as they played. She was strangely listless and came to life only when she caught herself darting her tongue out to lick at her lips. The taste of Lenn still lingered there.

"I'm worried about you, sport." Chris hunched over his coffee. Charlie and Vanessa had finally gone to bed a few minutes earlier, and it was obvious that he'd been waiting to talk without interference. "I know you said nothing was going on with you and Lenn, but I have my doubts. I saw the way he checked you out this afternoon. I know that look. For that matter, I saw the way you looked at him."

"Stop it. I'm old enough to take care of myself. I told you that."

"Sure. First that dimwit Brian, then Danny-boy, who's halfway to pushing up daisies, and now Lenn. You call that taking care of yourself?"

"Butt out of my life, Chris."

"I can't. You don't know Lenn like I do."

"Yeah, that's what's got me puzzled. You and he have been tight for years. Now you're running him down. I don't get it."

"You don't need to. Lenn's . . . well, there's a lot about Lenn you don't know. Reasons for the way he is."

"Then tell me."

"I can't, Katie." Chris looked torn. "Trust me. Lenn's not the kind of man who'll make a commitment. Not agai—" He stood up abruptly.

"Just one darn minute here. You were going to say 'not again,' weren't you?" Katie jumped up and followed her brother out of the dining room.

"Forget it. I gotta get going. Take my advice and stay clear of Lenn." He headed for the door.

"Chris," she called after him. "You can't leave without telling me what you're talking about."

"I can and I will. I may not want you seeing Lenn, but he's still my friend. The kind who sticks through thick and thin. I owe him, and I won't betray things he's told me. This is one time that insatiable curiosity of yours is going to have to go unsatisfied. Take my word for it. Lenn's not the kind of guy you should get mixed up with. For once in your life, listen to my advice." He planted a quick kiss on her cheek and bounded down the steps to his car.

"Chris? Damn it, Chris." She was talking to air. He pulled onto the street nearly as fast as Lenn had. If this kept up, there'd be more rubber on the driveway than cement.

Katie shivered against the soft evening breeze and turned angrily into the house. How could Chris leave her hanging like that? Men! He was as bad as Lenn with his secrets about Nicaragua. Katie absently flicked out the lights as she padded down the hall to her room.

Undressing in the dark, she slipped between lemon-fresh laundered sheets and glared at the stippled plaster on the ceiling for a long time before she slept.

Katie pushed open the door to the newsroom. One word, one smart-mouthed word, and she was headed straight for Sal's office to resign. And the only reason he was getting that much of a chance was because she had gotten awfully fond of the job. She liked cruising around town, listening to the police band on the van's radio. She liked finding out things firsthand. And she liked seeing photos she'd taken printed in the paper. But that was the only reason she was giving him a chance to shape up. She wasn't the slightest bit curious to know about his secret past. But he'd better not push, or she was out of there.

Two feet from her desk, she slammed to a stop. On the top of Lenn's monitor, a limp white napkin was taped to a straw which was stuck into a blue mound of Silly-Putty. Lenn was in his usual sprawl halfway across the aisle. The newspaper, folded to the half-done crossword, dangled from his hand. She met his eyes over the makeshift flag. He was wearing a look she'd seen many times in the past—the picture of a man contrite and anxious to make amends. She'd fallen for that look a hundred times and, damn her gullible soul, she was falling for it again.

With a heavy sigh of capitulation, she asked, "What we got today?"

Lenn straightened in his chair. "The union's settled. We got a follow-up."

"Well," she hitched her camera bag higher on her shoulder, "let's get to it."

It had been easier than he'd expected. Lenn gathered his gear and followed her out the door. But it was only a reprieve, and he knew it. He sure didn't intend to blow it by commenting on how delightfully she was wiggling along in front of him. Nope. She needed time to come to terms with what was happening between them. Hell, *he* needed time. But there wasn't anything saying he couldn't look a little while he was waiting. Shifting his waistband to adjust the fit of his jeans, he hoped it wasn't too long a wait.

The first couple of days, there was an awful lot of silence in the van. Then they started to talk. Well, *she* started to talk—hinting about Nicaragua, asking why he hadn't settled down, stuff like that. Some questions he evaded, some he answered—after a fashion. By Wednesday they were back to the occasional banter. He nagged her about her smoking. She countered that reformed weed addicts were unbearable to live with. It wouldn't be long before he could make his move.

Lenn was whistling when he sauntered out of the newsroom on Thursday evening.

"Where's Katie?"

"Darkroom," Lenn answered Sal without bothering to look up from the monitor.

"Get her. I phoned Ed. He's got a chopper waiting for you. Got wind there's a flood sweeping through Aguila Canyon."

Lenn stopped typing. "A flood?"

"Yeah. Don't know how bad it is. Could be it's just a leak." Sal shrugged his rounded shoulders.

Lenn reached for the phone and jabbed out the first number of the double digit for the darkroom. Hunching the receiver into the crook of his neck, he noticed Sal settling his ample bottom on the corner of his desk. He looked up, inquiring, "Anything else, Pop?"

"I was wonderin' how you and Katie were getting along these days."

"Pretty good, I guess."

"Just pretty good?"

"Yeah. What did you expect?"

Sal coughed, shifting his weight restlessly. "Nothin'. What I meant was, you guys aren't fighting so much anymore. Are you?"

Lenn quirked an eyebrow suspiciously. "We seem to be working out our differences. Why?"

"No reason. How's it going with, uh, what's her name, Jenna?"

"You mean the nice Italian girl Mama fixed me up with? The one who's supposed to make me think of settling down and raising bambinos?"

"Your mama only wants to see you happy."

"Yeah, well. I'm happy the way I am."

"So, how is Jenna?"

"Couldn't say. I'm not seeing her anymore." He rocked back in his chair. What on earth was with Pop today? He'd never taken an interest in his love life before.

"Well, then, what's the latest one's name?"

"Uh, there isn't one. What's with the third degree?"

"Just making small talk. Can't I be interested in my son?" Conjuring up an injured look, Sal slid off the desk. "Well, uh . . . I guess I'd better let you get to work. Later."

With a puzzled shake of his head, Lenn watched Sal rumble across the room, then dialed the other number of Katie's line. Making small talk, he echoed. When there was a flood to cover? That wasn't like Pop.

Katie's husky voice answered the phone and he forgot all about Sal.

"Uh uh, no way. I'm not getting into that thing." Katie had been so excited about the story that she hadn't paid much attention to their destination, not even when Lenn pulled into the small airfield. But when he hustled her toward a helicopter sitting on the tarmac, she realized that he expected her to get in that—that mechanical mosquito.

"Damn it, Katie, we don't have time to fool around. Come on." Lenn grabbed her arm, but she dug in her heels.

"I'm not fooling. I don't like flying. What's wrong with taking the van?"

"Into a flood?" he snapped sarcastically. "Last time I looked, it wasn't equipped with pontoons."

Katie balled her fists into her hips. "Well, neither is that."

"Yeah, but *that* can fly over a flood. The van can't. Come on."

"I'm not going. Here." She thrust her camera bag at him. "You take the pictures. I'll wait here."

Lenn shoved the bag back onto her shoulder. "Look . . ." He spoke slowly, enunciating each word as if she were some sort of idiot. "I can't take decent pictures while I'm standing on the ground, let alone while I'm flying a chopper."

"Wait a minute. What do you mean, *you're* flying the chopper?"

"Just that." He herded her to the side of the aircraft. She looked nervously up at the rotors, which were mercifully still.

"Now, get your tail into that seat and buckle in." He tossed his pack through the open side into the backseat. "Or do you want me to heft you in?"

He would, too. "Listen, Lenn." She tried to reason with him. "Remember, I told you I was afraid of flying?"

"Yeah. I also seem to remember you babbling on about how a person can overcome his fears. Practice what you preach and get your cute little fanny in there." He thrust his hips forward and hunkered his shoulders down to look her in the eye. His voice softened slightly. "I thought you were all fired up to take pictures of the flood. Thought you were anxious to see it firsthand, up close."

He fought dirty. She did want to see what was

happening in the canyon. "But that thing doesn't even have any doors. What if I fall out?"

"The doors have been taken off so you can take pictures without the plexiglass interfering," he explained, "and that's what the harness is for. Trust me, you won't fall out."

"Trust you? Hah!" How many times had she heard *that*? She cast a wary glance into the cockpit. There wasn't even a steering wheel. Just some stupid joystick like a giant video game. "You sure you know how to fly that thing?" she asked hesitantly.

He nodded.

"Like you knew how to ride that dirt bike?" She managed a wan smile, but her stomach fluttered nervously.

"Yeah. I didn't let you fall off then, did I?"

"No, but the wheels stayed on the ground."

"Most of the time." He grinned. "Come on, Katie. Where's that gutsy broad who's been giving me what for these last few weeks? Or have you gone back to being the wimp you used to be when we were kids?"

"Wimp! Damn you, Domina, I'm no wimp."

"Oh, yeah? You were scared of the dark," he ticked off a finger, "scared of snakes," another finger counted off, "scared of lightning, scared of spiders, scared of your own shadow. I thought you'd grown up some, but it looks like I was wrong."

"I'm not like that anymore."

"Prove it," he challenged. "Get into that cockpit and strap in. I'm going to do the preflight check. We've wasted enough time on your ridiculous hangups." He pivoted on a heel and headed toward the back end of the aircraft.

Hangups. She didn't have any hangups. Well, maybe a few teeny-weeny ones. She'd show Lenn-smart-ass-Domina. She'd grit her teeth one more time and get in there and show him. She was *not* a wimp. Hiking her camera bag higher onto her shoulder, she started around the front of the helicopter.

"Other side, Katie. The pilot sits on the right."

With a scathing scowl in Lenn's direction, she stalked back to where she'd been and pulled herself into the cockpit.

Lenn smothered an outright chuckle at Katie struggling into the chopper. For a minute there, he'd thought his goading tactic wasn't going to work. She really was scared. But she'd picked up a lot of spunk since she was a kid. With a wry shake of his head, he switched his attention to the chopper and began his walkaround.

"Where'd you learn?"

Lenn jerked up, barely missing the tail section he had ducked beneath. "Damn it, Katie, what are you doing out here? Get back in that cockpit."

"Uh uh, I'm not getting in until you tell me where and how you learned to fly."

"Katie, we don't have time for a history of my flying experience." He tried to ignore her and concentrate on checking out the Jet Ranger.

"Well, I'm not going up with you until I know you can really fly this thing. So you might as well talk to me," she said with a determined set to her features.

Lenn closed his eyes in exasperation. He was only too familiar with that look. She meant what she said.

"All right," he sighed. "After I finished school in Italy, I bummed around Europe. Mainly because

I didn't want to come home. I felt my family had rejected me, so I was going to reject them. I took whatever work turned up and eventually got a job as a guide for a small heli-skiing outfit in the Italian Alps. The guy who owned it was one heck of a skier, and even though he was quite a bit older, we became pretty good friends. He's still a good buddy.'' He smiled at the memory of Tony and his infinite patience with the brash, cocky kid he'd taken under his wing. ''Anyway, to make a long story short, whenever nothing else was going on, he taught me to fly. I kinda got into it. Took some formal training, then went back and worked for Tony for about two years as a pilot. We had some great times. I loved flying, not to mention all that free skiing.''

Katie tilted her head and looked at him with those probing green eyes. ''How come you quit?''

''One of the guys who skied regularly was a newsman. Talked about the stories he was involved in all the time. One day I faced the facts. I wanted to do the kind of things he was doing. Oh, I loved flying. But even if printer's ink wasn't legitimately in my blood, somewhere along the line Sal must have instilled the love of the business in me.'' He paused, trying to sort his reasons, his feelings. ''I guess I finally realized that by rejecting everything Sal stood for, I was only hurting myself. I worked for Tony until I had enough money to take a journalism course in London, and the rest, as they say, is history. Now that I've satisfied your nosy streak, how about getting in the chopper and letting me get back to my check? At this rate, the flood will probably be a dry wash by the time we get to it.''

Katie wasn't all that crazy about following Lenn's

instructions, but she'd used every stalling tactic she could think of. Trotting back to the cockpit, she hauled herself in. It took some fumbling to figure out the seat belt that was more like a harness than the car type she was familiar with. But by the time Lenn finished with whatever fiddling around he was doing out there and had joined her, she had the contraption securely in place. She took a peek at the gaping door beside her. She didn't feel one bit safer.

"Here. Put these on." Lenn handed her a set of headphones. "They'll muffle some of the sound, and we can talk to each other through the mikes."

Katie plopped the headset over her springy curls. Not only was she about to die, she was going to have to do it with flat hair. She was going to look awful when they opened the coffin.

Oh, Lord, she was really going through with this—but nobody said she had to watch. She closed her eyes and waited. And waited. She opened her eyes.

"Uh, Lenn, why are we still sitting here?" She squinted at him suspiciously. Was he deliberately trying to make her crazy by prolonging her agony?

Lenn expelled a frustrated puff of air. "I'm doing a preflight check."

Katie knew there was something wrong with the helicopter and he wasn't telling her. "I thought that's what you just did out there."

"That was an exterior check, this is an instrument check. It's routine."

"Oh." That was good, wasn't it? It showed that he was cautious. That he knew what he was doing. She watched him as he efficiently examined the instruments and controls.

It was crazy. She didn't trust Lenn as far as she could throw him. She was petrified of flying, yet somehow the fact that he was the pilot made her feel a tiny bit more secure.

Finally he pressed a button that started a low whine. As the rotors picked up speed, Lenn pulled on a lever between them and the helicopter started to vibrate. Katie felt as if she was in a washing machine, and the army of moths that must have been hibernating in the roll she'd had for breakfast began battering themselves silly on the walls of her stomach. Oh, God, the whole thing was going to shake apart, and she'd be sitting on her fanny on the tarmac with a pile of metal and bolts all around her. Lenn didn't look the slightest bit worried, but then he always had been a little crazy. Katie clutched her bag tighter—there was nothing else to hold onto. She was giving serious thought to saying to heck with Lenn and bailing out when the helicopter lifted off the ground, and it was too late.

"Tower, this is November 6233 Sierra." Lenn held the chopper steady about four feet off the ground.

"November 6233 Sierra. Roger. Go ahead." The radio crackled a reply.

"Request clearance for take-off from west side of ramp, northbound."

Katie listened as the tower gave Lenn wind and altimeter information and cleared them for departure. Lenn actually sounded as if he knew what he was doing. She took a deep breath—and for a short minute she felt slightly better. Then the helicopter started to move, speeding forward without raising much higher into the air than the hover Lenn had been holding. The nose tipped downward. Katie heard a moaning mewl and knew it had come from somewhere down in her throat. The cockpit began to shudder. Oh, Lord, they were going to crash! Then suddenly, the helicopter rose gracefully into the air. Her stomach, however, did not. She tried to tell herself to be grateful that she'd left those blasted moths behind, only she wasn't too happy about the gnawing void that had taken their place.

Swallowing convulsively, she hazarded a quick peek at the ground. The airfield, scattered with light airplanes and other helicopters, gradually grew smaller, but really, Katie thought, it wasn't much worse than peering out of the window of a very tall building. Except for the missing door. "Hey, this isn't as bad as I thought it would be."

Lenn flashed that set of pearly-whites at her. And if he weren't wearing those snazzy aviator sunglasses, she was sure she'd be able to detect an I-told-you-so glint in the dark depths of those black eyes of his. Fortunately, he had the sense not to voice the words.

By the time they neared the sight of the flooding, Katie had gained enough courage to take out her equipment and make a few test readings on her light meter.

It was an aquatic hell below. For the first time, she felt safe in the air. The cockpit was a relative haven compared to the insane cascade of water pouring through the canyon.

As she snapped pictures from every angle, she guessed that somewhere around fifteen to twenty vacation homes had been situated along the banks of the river before the flood had gushed through. One cabin had been literally washed from its foundations, others had only peaks of roofs to show where they were. Here and there, Katie could see people scrambling to higher ground. She tried not to think that there were some who might not have made it. Lenn told her rescue teams were on the way, but she couldn't see any sign of them.

"Lenn, can you set the chopper down? I'd like to get some closer shots." She had become slightly more comfortable with this flying business, but she wasn't yet at the stage where she could lean out of the door for a better angle—and it was unlikely she ever would be.

"Katie, look around. Do you see any spots I could land?"

He had a point. The only area not covered in roiling brown water was crowded with dark, reaching trees. Katie had resigned herself to strictly aerial views, when Lenn added, "But I can hover as low as you want. Will that do you?"

"Why didn't you say that in the first place? Can you get close to that house over there?" She pointed. "The one where the water's broken through the window?"

For an answer, Lenn swooped down closer and held the chopper steady near the window she'd indicated, letting her get a perfect photo. Next, at her request, he skimmed alongside a road grader that was being carried along the raging torrent as if it were a Tonka toy floating in a child's bath.

Lenn deftly piloted the aircraft wherever Katie instructed, and she was almost on the verge of admitting that she was beginning to enjoy herself when they spotted the children. They were clinging desperately to a large log that was wedged against a pile of rocks.

"Where the hell are those rescue choppers? That log's not going to hold for very long."

Katie craned her neck in every possible direction. The sky was ominously empty.

"We're going to have to get them off. Undo your harness."

"What?" Katie gaped at Lenn.

"You're going to have to go out onto the skids and get those kids. I'll hold her as close as I can."

"Lenn, I can't do that."

"You can. You have to."

Katie looked at the screaming children, a boy about six and a little girl who couldn't be more than four. On the south shore, too far to be of any help, a small clutch of people were straining to hold back a frantic woman whose screams were lost in the roar of the water and the beat of the rotors. What choice did she have? She swallowed the fear that rose in her throat and nodded, undoing her belt while Lenn lowered the helicopter and brought it to a suspended standstill a scant foot above the muddy, swirling water.

"Do the harness back up and hook your arm into the loop. That'll give you a little mobility as well as something to hold onto."

Obeying his instructions, she took a short second to direct a silent prayer heavenward, inhaled a deep breath, and stepped cautiously onto the skid, trying to ignore how narrow it was. She hoped the coil of the headphone would extend far enough. The last thing she wanted to do was to take it off and lose contact with Lenn's calming words.

"That's it, Katie, you're doing fine."

The grinding whir of the blades mingled with the children's terrified screams, the rush of the angry river, and the thundering of her own heart. The bitter metallic taste of fear was in her mouth, making her ill to the point of nausea. She pulled in another steadying breath and crouched toward the children as far as the harness would allow. The little girl was closest but still several crucial inches away. If only the child would reach up to her, but she was too frightened to let go of the log.

Katie needed those extra inches. Straightening, she unhooked her elbow from the harness and grabbed the strap with her hand. With the extra foot she'd gained, she managed to encircle the girl under her arms and lift her up. Shouting to be heard above the rotors, she coaxed the girl to grab onto her neck. Luckily, the child's panicked reaction was to do that very thing. Katie inched her way back toward the door. Lenn's face tightened in concentration as he held the chopper steady. She tried to maneuver the child into the cockpit, but the terrified girl wouldn't release her hold.

"You're going to have to get in with her." Lenn noticed her struggle with the child. "Once she's inside, maybe she'll feel safe enough to let go so you can get the boy."

Easier said than done, she thought, trying to balance the weight of the child as she edged into the cockpit.

"Hurry, Katie, the log's shifting." She heard Lenn bite off an imprecation as she fell into the seat. He pulled the chopper up and back just as the log broke loose from the rocks.

"Lenn. It's headed toward that boulder!"

"I see it. Damn, the kid'll be smashed to smithereens if it hits at the speed it's going." Lenn raced the helicopter along the water, quickly overtaking the careening log. "We've only got one chance. I have to put the chopper down on the boulder and try to grab the kid when the log hits."

"Lenn, that's impossible."

She looked over the small wet head huddled against her. The boulder seemed awfully small. It rose above the swirling water roughly five or six feet and was about ten feet wide and a few feet longer in jagged length, but at least it was relatively level. Even if they could land—and now that she'd seen Lenn in action, she didn't doubt he could set the chopper on the rock—how could he get the boy?

"Got any better ideas?" Lenn already had the chopper in a hover a few feet above the boulder. Instinctively, she hugged the sobbing girl closer and braced against the force of the landing, shuddering at the grinding scrape of the skids against bare rock. She held her breath for several aching seconds, waiting for the helicopter to skitter wildly into the water below. When the chopper held its precarious perch, she expelled the air from her lungs in one long, wrenching sigh.

Lenn stopped only to undo his harness and rip off his headphone. He was out of the chopper and over the edge of the rock before Katie managed to clamber out her door. With the girl perched on her hip, she peered over the edge. Lenn was chest-deep in water, using a jutting rock as a handhold. The log was headed directly toward him. Her breath caught deep in her chest. As the point of the tree hit the boulder only inches to the left of him, Lenn plucked the boy away, turning to protect the child as he used his hold on the rock to pull them partially up the boulder.

"Lenn!" Katie screamed as the log pivoted sideways and smashed against his lower body.

He shouted something back at her, but the words were lost in the wind and chop of the helicopter blades. She watched helplessly as he tried to use his legs to push the log away. Finally, aided by the force of the current, the log broke free to sluice past the boulder. Lenn sagged against the side of the rock for a long moment before he tried to climb back up. The lower part of the boulder was slick, battered by water, and Lenn slipped dangerously more than once.

Katie knelt at the edge, coaxing the girl to release her hold so she could lie on her stomach and reach for the boy. She yelled Lenn's name. He saw her outstretched arms and manipulated the boy up toward her. Grabbing his reaching arms, she pulled him to safety, enfolding him and the girl into her arms. Though both children were wet and frightened, they seemed otherwise unhurt as they clung to each other and to her. Moments later, Lenn heaved himself over the edge and collapsed beside her. Katie sobbed with relief.

Over Lenn's huddled form, she saw the people on the far shore. The woman who had been so agitated was curled into the arms of one of her companions. She was obviously the children's mother, and Katie waved an arm to indicate that they were safe. But how Lenn was going to reunite them, she didn't know.

Lowering her gaze to meet Lenn's, she read the sheer exhaustion etched on his face. "Thanks," he mouthed, not even trying to compete with the noise of the rotors.

Thanks? *He* was thanking *her*. All she'd done was pull the boy up after Lenn had saved him. He was the one who should be earning thanks. He'd risked his life.

Katie's throat constricted against the well of tears trapped there. She reached a hand to wipe the water from his cheek. Lenn bent his head to the side, trapping her fingers in the crook of his shoulder. For a long moment they sat that way, neither wanting to break their silent bond.

Finally, Lenn cocked his head toward the chopper. "We'd better get these kids to safety," he shouted. Struggling to a crouch, he hefted the boy into his arms and carried him to the aircraft. Depositing him in the front passenger seat and strapping him in, he motioned for Katie to get in back with the girl.

It was then she noticed the bleeding gash on Lenn's thigh.

"Lenn, your leg."

He heard her shout but shook it off. "Forget it. We've got to get these kids out of here." Coaxing the girl out of Katie's arms, he slid his pack onto the floor and secured her into the backseat. "Damn it, Katie, get in here and strap in," he yelled, before moving round to slide into the pilot seat. He hooked his headphone onto his head and Katie quickly did the same.

"Lenn, you need to do something about that leg."

"I said, forget it, Katie. It's okay." Lenn sent her a quelling glare over the seat as he leaned over and adjusted a headphone to fit the little boy. When he had it in place, he asked, "How ya doin', tiger? Ever been in a chopper before?"

Wide-eyed, the boy shook his head.

Katie felt a tug on her sleeve and looked down at a pair of the biggest, bluest eyes she had ever seen. A chubby little hand handed her a set of headphones. She smiled at the determined little face and adjusted the headset as much as possible. Placing the receiver on the small wet head, she tried not to laugh as the earpieces dropped around the tiny girl's neck. The girl stubbornly lifted her little arms and held them in place.

"Hey, sweetie, how's it going back there?" Lenn looked over his shoulder at the girl.

" 'Kay." She looked at Lenn, then back up at Katie. "I want my mommy."

"Well, sweetie, I can't get to where your mommy is, but there are some other helicopters coming that'll be able to pick her up and take her to the same place we'll be taking you. How's that sound?"

" 'Kay, I . . . I guess."

"Hey, how about telling me your name? I can't keep calling you sweetie, 'cause my girlfriend there might get jealous."

A faint smile touched her little porcelain-doll mouth. "Mandy."

"That's a pretty name. What's yours, tiger?"

"He my brother. Him Chad." The little girl piped up before her obviously shyer brother managed an answer.

"Well, Chad, I guess you're my co-pilot for this flight. That okay with you?"

"Um . . . yeah, I guess."

"Your job will be to keep an eye on that dial

there. It's called an altimeter, and when it reaches 2,000, I want you to let me know. Okay?''

He waited for the enthusiastic nod, then expertly lifted the chopper into the air just as the first of the rescue craft appeared on the horizon. Katie listened while he made contact with the choppers on an emergency frequency that he told Chad was called "guard." Explaining their situation, he learned where the flood victims were to be taken, and set his course accordingly.

They'd been in the air for fifteen minutes before Katie realized she hadn't taken a single shot of what was probably the most dramatic rescue of the day.

EIGHT

"Damn it, Lenn," Katie harangued as they headed back to the helicopter. "Why on earth didn't you let them look at that leg."

He was limping badly. Behind the blood-soaked tatter of denim, the gash in his leg, though no longer bleeding profusely, was raw and ugly.

"Listen, Katie," he growled. "There were at least ten people in there who needed attention a whole lot worse than I did. A doctor wouldn't have gotten to me for ages. Anyway, all this needs is a little antiseptic and it'll be fine."

"It needs more than a little antiseptic. And what's your all-fired hurry? You dropped Mandy and Chad off as if they were hot potatoes. You didn't even wait for the rescue team to bring in their mother. I'm sure she would have liked to thank you. And if we'd waited, there'd have been more than enough time for someone to see to your leg." Katie was so busy tearing into Lenn that she got into the helicopter without the slightest hesitation.

"That's exactly why I didn't stick around. I don't need any thanks. I didn't do anything anyone else wouldn't have done."

"But the point is, it was *you* who did it," Katie shouted, but her words were lost in the roar of the rotors when Lenn started the helicopter. Muttering a couple of succinct words, she grabbed her headphone, slammed it on her head, and continued her tirade.

"Enough," Lenn snapped. "I did what I had to do. It's over. We're going to get the story filed, and then we're going to forget it."

"*Fine*. But first we stop and have that leg looked at."

"No way. I'm not going to any hospital."

"But it could get infected," she insisted.

"Not if it's cleaned properly, but to make you happy, we'll stop at my apartment and you can fix it up."

"I don't know anything about dressing a wound that size."

"Nothing to it. I'll tell you what to do."

Katie waited in the living room while Lenn went into his bedroom to remove his torn jeans. She paced from one gray wall to the other, inspecting the colorful prints of antique cars that dotted the apartment while she tried to figure out what they said about the bloody obstinate man who'd bought them. Did his taste in pictures mean that he was basically an old-fashioned man at heart? Katie shook her head at the fanciful thought. It was more likely that he'd gotten the whole lot for a good price at a flea market. Now, *that* felt more like the case. Actually—she looked around the room—the only thing that really seemed like Lenn was the collection of cacti over in the corner. Prickly. Now *that* was Lenn.

Except that the man who came back into the room didn't look prickly at all. He was wearing a white terry robe tied at the waist. The top gaped open above the knot, and the dark hair sprinkling his tanned chest looked soft and springy, inviting her to touch. Definitely not prickly. She reined in the wayward urge.

"Are you ready to amputate?" He handed her a roll of bandages, a bottle of antiseptic, and a wad of cotton.

"Don't tempt me." Katie tried to remain indifferent as Lenn flopped onto the sofa and flipped the robe aside to expose his wound. He'd already washed the majority of the dried blood from his sturdy, muscled thigh. She shivered, and not only because of the ugly slash and blotches of darkening bruises that marred his flesh. "Darn it, Lenn. I really wish you'd let me take you into a hospital. You've lost a lot of blood and that really should have stitches."

"Why? So the scar I'm going to have anyway will be prettier? Look, that doesn't matter to me. Just put some antiseptic on it and wrap it up," he instructed impatiently.

Katie opened the bottle and saturated the wad of cotton, trying hard to concentrate on the wound instead of the firm muscle that surrounded it.

"Pretty ugly, isn't it?"

Without thinking, she answered, "I wouldn't say that. Uh, I mean . . ."

"Katie?" He bent his head trying to look into her lowered eyes. "Are you blushing? What *is* going through that pretty little head of yours?"

Without meeting his probing gaze, she dabbed the soaked cotton directly onto his wound. He growled a colorful four-letter word and caught her hand before she could inflict further punishment.

"Easy, love—that hurts."

"Sorry," she muttered. "I wasn't thinking."

"What you really mean is that you were thinking too much. I do believe you're not as unaffected by me as you'd like me to believe."

"This is going to hurt a lot more if you don't get off my case, Lenn."

He didn't say anything to that, but she knew without looking that he was wearing that smug, knowing grin of his. With exaggerated care, she bandaged his leg to his satisfaction, then breathed a heartfelt sigh of relief when he vanished into the bedroom to change. He reappeared minutes later, slightly more decent in a pair of gray jogging pants and a white sweatshirt. Unfortunately, even fully clothed, he still looked disgustingly sexy.

"You hungry, Red?" he asked. "For food, I mean?"

She decided to ignore that. "Yeah, come to think of it, I am."

"How about some of yesterday's pizza?"

"Sounds good. I hope there's a lot. I'm so famished I could eat a horse."

"Yeah?" he beamed. "Well, there's a little of that on it, too." He headed for the kitchen with Katie trailing behind.

She watched him zap the pizza in the microwave

and couldn't stop herself from remembering the last time she'd been in Lenn's apartment. He'd been a different man that night. A man not at all like the carefree one who was puttering around the small kitchen today. He was acting as if nothing had ever happened between them. In fact, he'd acted that way all week. Well, that was fine with her. She certainly wasn't going to bring up *that* fiasco.

"Where'd you get this?" she asked through her first bite of the best pizza she'd ever sunk her teeth into. "It's great."

"I made it, of course. Where else would a good Italian get pizza?"

"Mario's down the block?" she said smartly.

"You wound me. Here I was figuring I'd impressed you with my culinary expertise." He pulled a hard-done-by look that Katie remembered vividly from the stock of faces he'd used when he was a teenager, and she couldn't help but laugh.

But beneath the laughter she had to admit that she was impressed. Oh, not so much by the fact he could cook. These days most swinging bachelors out to dazzle the ladies usually could. What had impressed her was what he'd done that afternoon. He had risked his life to save those children, and though it might be true, as he said, that others might have done the same, it wasn't only his heroics she'd noticed but the way he'd acted with Mandy and Chad. And if she were to really think about it, the way he had acted with her. She didn't have to think for very long to recognize that he'd deliberately goaded her into forgetting her fears.

Munching another slice of pizza, she tried to fit

the bits and pieces she was learning about him into a neat character puzzle, but the pieces were rough-edged and wouldn't fit. She'd give her trusty Nikon if she could get him to open up and tell her about his life—about what had made him into the man he now was. Because she finally had to admit he was no longer the annoying nemesis he'd been as a boy. Oh, he worked hard at making people believe he was still the devil-may-care renegade he'd always been, but she was beginning to believe it was a cover. He was hiding a part of himself, maybe even running away from something.

"Why are you staring at me like that?" Lenn wiped his fingers on a paper towel and wadded it into a ball.

"I'm trying to figure you out." She opted for the truth.

"What's to figure?" Avoiding her eyes, he piled the plates together and headed for the sink.

"A lot, I think." She didn't bother getting up to help him, suspecting he'd growl that just because he'd hurt his leg it didn't mean he was an invalid. "What happened in Nicaragua, Lenn?"

"Nothing." He didn't look up, but she saw him stiffen. "I've already told you enough. There's nothing more to talk about."

"I think there is. You're running from something. I want to know what."

"I'm not running from anything." He turned and skewered her with those flashing black eyes. "But if I were, it would be from you, lady. Go poke into someone else's past. Mine's not up for grabs." He slapped down the dishes and hobbled angrily out the door.

"Lenn." She bolted after him. "I didn't mean—"

"Look, Katie, I don't really give a damn what you *meant*. I'm going to work. You coming or not?"

Katie cringed inwardly as she followed him out the door. *Now you've done it, O'Brien. You'll be lucky if he ever speaks to you again.*

Lenn spoke, all right. But only the bare words necessary to get their story done, then he limped her out to her car, got into his Corvette, and drove off into the night.

The weekend seemed about two days longer than normal, mostly because she spent it thinking about Lenn, wondering about the feelings she was starting to have for him. Forced to recognize a tender, fragile caring that was starting to wrap around her heart like a fine, delicate web of angel hair, she knew she had to help him break free of whatever held him in its grip. Because no matter how much he denied it, there was something eating at his gut. She could keep probing and he could keep fighting her, and that could go on forever. Or she could be there, waiting patiently for him to trust her, but she realized that, too, could take forever. It didn't matter.

She wasn't sure why, but she was not giving up on Lenn.

Katie sauntered into work on Monday morning half an hour late—on purpose. For some perverse reason she couldn't for the life of her fathom, she wanted to bug Lenn.

He wasn't there.

She fumed at her desk for nearly fifteen minutes before Sal walked out of his office, stopping abruptly when he noticed her. He slammed a pudgy hand into the middle of his forehead. "Oh, Katie, I forgot to call you to tell you that you didn't have to come in until Lenn gets back."

"Until Lenn gets back?" she echoed. "Where's Lenn?" The rotten skunk hadn't told her he was going anywhere.

"You mean your dad didn't tell you?"

"No, what was he supposed to tell me?" she inquired, wondering if maybe it hadn't been such a great idea to unplug the phone for the entire weekend because she hadn't felt like talking to anyone.

"Lenn's in the hospital."

"What?"

"Yeah, that leg he hurt on Friday kept opening up on him. Gio went over yesterday morning to take him some of her homemade pasta and he could barely stand, he'd lost so much blood. She hustled him off to the hospital. They gave him a transfusion and sewed him up. They're going to keep the stupid fool in there for a couple of days."

She'd told him he should have had it looked at. "What hospital?"

The name had barely left Sal's mouth when Katie spun out of the newsroom without even a good-bye. She didn't want to admit it, but if anything happened to him, it would leave a big black hole in her life. The last couple of weeks had been the most exciting she'd ever known. Now, suddenly, she had to face the realization that she didn't want it to end.

She lit into him the instant she charged into his room. "You see! I told you to have it looked at right away, but *no-o-o*, you had to do it your own stupid way. Now look where you are."

"What?" Lenn managed a groggy tilt to one corner of his mouth. "No flowers?"

"Damn you," she whispered sharply, slipping her small hand into his. "Why are you so hard on yourself?"

His eyes roamed the room. "You call this hard? I get room service, maid service, and a pretty little nurse to feel my leg every hour or so . . ."

"You've been drugged."

"Yeah, I know . . ." Letting his lids drift shut, he dropped his head back onto the sterile white pillow.

He was a rumpled, seductive mess with his dark, unruly hair clinging to his forehead. A long plastic tube linked him to an IV bottle hanging beside his bed, and he wore a pale-blue hospital gown that she was certain he had objected to strenuously. He looked so . . . vulnerable? She peeled the damp strands of hair away from his head and asked, "Are you in a lot of pain?"

He smiled languidly, opening his eyes to gaze up at her. "Nah, I don't feel a thing. Don't tell me you're concerned?"

"What kind of question is that?"

He shrugged, shifting to lift himself a little higher onto the pillow. His grip on her hand tightened involuntarily as pain sawed through his bones, making a liar out of him.

She winced. "You are in pain, aren't you?"

"No," he snapped. "I'm having an orgasm. Of course I'm in pain, Red. But I'll get over it. Is there any water on that table?"

"Yeah." Katie poured him a cup from the pitcher. She didn't think he was in any shape to sit up further, so she leaned forward and held the cup to his lips. His dark gaze shot straight down the front of her V-neck sweater. "Nice view, honey," he murmured sleepily. "Very nice."

"Down, boy." She straightened quickly. "You're in a hospital bed, remember?"

"So? The nurse won't be around for another twenty minutes or so. We've got time for a quickie."

"You're in no condition to even be thinking about sex. Now drink, before I pour this down your shorts," she threatened before setting the cup back on the table. If he was in good enough shape to proposition her, he was in good enough shape to manage on his own.

He grinned. "I'm not wearing any. Wanna see?" He made a move to throw back the covers.

"Don't bother." She caught his hand. "I already had a good laugh when I watched cartoons before breakfast. When are you getting out of here?"

"You missing me, by any chance?"

"Not likely," she lied.

"Well, just in case. I'll be out Wednesday, maybe even tomorrow, if I'm a good boy. Wanna have dinner?"

She wanted to say yes, she really did, but she didn't want to set herself up for a long, hard fall. Chris's warning played in the back of her head. "No, I've got a date Wednesday. In fact, I'm booked solid from then until the year 2000."

"Well, in that case, I'll make sure I'm out of here tomorrow."

"Dan's coming over," she hastily improvised.

A nerve twitched along his jaw. "I'll be over at six."

"I said Dan'll be there. Three's a crowd."

"Then he'll have to leave. I intend—"

"Excuse me?" A soft voice interrupted from the doorway. Katie whirled to see a raven-haired beauty stroll—no, *slink* into the room.

"Hello, Jenna." Lenn greeted the woman politely. Stiffly, it seemed to Katie. She had to hold herself in check not to raise a questioning eyebrow.

"Nice of you to drop by. I'd like you to meet my photographer, Katie O'Brien. Katie, Jenna Ferriero, a, er . . . friend."

Katie checked her out in a quick, single glance. She was tall, thin, and cover-girl beautiful. Not a hair out of place, not a single crease in her pencil-slim skirt. Katie tried not to think of her own faded jeans as she smiled at the woman and said, "Hello."

Jenna brushed past her with a very insincere, "How do you do?" and bent over to kiss Lenn full on the mouth. They exchanged a few words in rapid Italian. Lenn appeared more than a little irritated.

"How did you get here?" he asked in English.

"Your mother drove me," Jenna replied, reaching over to smooth back the hair on his forehead. "She's gone to pick up your sisters. They'll be here in about a half hour."

"I see." Lenn twisted his head away from her touch, so instead of mauling his face, she pulled up the sheet and started tucking it around him. He was about to explode, Katie thought. She'd seen that expression more than once.

She was right.

"For the love of— Jenna, will you stop mothering me!"

Katie backed toward the door, feeling distinctly

muttered behind the hand she had cupped over the receiver.

"No can do. Be there in about twenty minutes. *Ciao*."

The line went dead before she could say another word. And there were a lot she would have liked to spew into his stubborn ear. She mentally ran through a few before she decided to heck with it. Let him come. He'd see for himself that she wasn't available.

After all, wasn't that why she'd really invited Dan over?

She looked guiltily over at Dan sitting primly in his formal business suit at one end of her couch. She knew she shouldn't be using him that way, but the small remorse she felt evaporated quickly when she remembered how pompous he was. He hadn't even loosened his tie.

"Who was that?" Mr. Pompous wanted to know.

Forcing an unconcerned smile to her lips, she strolled back and set the phone on the end table. "Lenn. He's coming over."

"Good," he barked. "I intend to give him a piece of my mind about the hours you've been putting in."

"Uh, I wouldn't do that if I were you."

"And why not?"

"Because he's likely to tear your head off your shoulders," she warned. "He's kind of temperamental."

"Yeah, well, most wops are. He doesn't scare me." Dan stuck his chest out like a banty rooster.

Katie would have laughed if she hadn't blown a fuse. "How dare you! Where do you get off calling one of my friends a wop?" If she'd had something in her hand, she'd have thrown it.

"Oh, so now he's your *friend*. What's going on between you two, anyway? Maybe that crack over the phone the other day wasn't the joke you claimed."

"Just what are you implying?" Katie clenched her fists by her side.

"Maybe you've been doing more than work on those late nights."

"What! Why you . . . you . . ."

Oblivious to the sauce hitting the fan in Katie's apartment, Lenn whistled his way down Sunset Boulevard in the slow-crawling traffic. The sleek yellow hood of his cherished Corvette gleamed in the low glow of the late-afternoon sun. He hadn't been spending much time with Marilyn lately. He patted her dashboard affectionately. She probably understood. Cars weren't like women. They didn't put up a fuss when a man looked at another car with a better body. Though he had to admit, not many had a better body than Marilyn.

A vision flashed in his brain. Katie's body wiggling along in front of him as it had so often in the past couple of weeks. Yep, now there was a body. Not that Marilyn need be jealous. You couldn't really compare the two.

Funny, he managed to work with Katie every day, except for weekends, for two whole weeks. Adding the hours up in his head, he figured they'd spent about sixty hours together—more time than he'd spent with any woman with the exception of those in his family. And, of course, Suzanna.

No, damn it, no! He couldn't think about her now. He'd been thinking about the past too much lately.

It was over. Done. He had to forget it. Think about Katie.

He concentrated on trying to figure what there was about her that made him keep coming back. Probably the challenge of trying to get her into his bed. Yeah, that was it. He'd better remedy that little matter downright soon. Apart from wanting her so badly his belly ached with it, he was starting to get too close to her. He couldn't afford that. What he needed was to take her to bed and get her out of his system. Because there was no way he was going to let anyone get that close again. Not after Suzanna.

"You're asking me to leave because I called that . . . that Italian stallion a wop?" Dan howled, his face red with indignation.

"You're darn tootin' I am," Katie seethed, brushing her hair out of her eyes. They were standing practically nose to nose. "After what you said, you can just take your small, prejudiced mind—"

The doorbell chimed, entirely too pleasantly to match the heated atmosphere of the room.

"There's your *company*," Dan sneered.

"Can it, Dan. You've said enough." She brushed past him and flung open the door.

Lenn stood there wearing a nauseating smile and his pleated white pants with a soft cream-colored shirt unbuttoned at the collar. A white tie hung loosely around his neck, the knot resting halfway down his chest. His arms were full of roses.

She was in no mood for roses, or for the too-disgustingly-good-looking man who was holding them. She hadn't asked him here. In fact, she'd made it clear he wasn't wanted. And neither was the idiot behind her.

Lenn ignored her unwelcoming glare and moved past her into the room. Spying Dan, steaming but still unruffled, he muttered, "Oh, oh."

"Come right in, why don't you?" She dripped sarcasm. The two clods deserved each other. "Dan, Lenn. Lenn, Dan." Her hand ping-ponged from one to the other as she drilled out the introductions. "Go to it. I'm going to the kitchen for a good stiff drink."

"Well, I'm leaving," Dan huffed, storming past Lenn and out into the hall.

Katie stuck her head out the door and yelled after him, "Good bloody riddance!" and felt unaccountably lighter, freer.

"Holy smokes." Lenn watched Katie slam the door and seal it with a kick. "What was that all about?"

"Nothing." She flounced into the kitchen.

Lenn trailed behind. "Didn't look like nothing from where I was standing. Sounds like you two had a bit of a disagreement. A permanent one, I hope?"

Katie squinted over her shoulder with an I-don't-want-to-talk-about-it-and-it's-none-of-your-business look, all the while struggling to open a bottle of rum.

"If you want to take care of these," he waggled the flowers in his hand, "I'll get that."

Katie whisked the roses out of his grasp and rammed open a cupboard door, searching for a vase. Lenn might have been hurt by her rough treatment of his admittedly calculated offering if he hadn't been raised in a family of volatile Italian women. He smiled as he poured the drinks. She needed to let off a little steam.

Glasses in hand, he sauntered into the living room and settled on the couch. Katie stomped after him and slammed the vase of fragrant-smelling buds onto the coffee table, then proceeded to charge around the room bashing nonexistent lumps out of every cushion in sight.

Sipping his rum and Coke, he smugly enjoyed the fact that he was the one who was sitting on her sofa while Dan had been tossed out on his ear. He allowed a timed, ten minutes of nonstop bitching, agreeing completely with the string of adjectives she used to describe his rival, but at the same time discounting completely the choice terms she flailed at him for having the temerity to show up after she'd ordered otherwise.

"Enough," he tried for stern, hoping his true amusement wasn't apparent. "Calm down before you get heat stroke."

She fastened a glare on him that would have cowed a lesser man.

"Have your drink before the ice melts. We really should get a move on. Our reservation's for seven." Lenn held his breath.

Katie marched up to the coffee table where Lenn had set her drink and picked it up, fully intending to down it in one fast I'll-show-him gulp, when she suddenly realized how silly she was being.

She was well rid of Dan, and she knew it. And she was, though she hated to admit it, pleased that Lenn had showed. This was probably going to be the stupidest thing she had ever done in her entire life, but darn if she didn't want to spend the evening with him. On her own terms, of course.

"Pretty sure of yourself, aren't you?"

"Yeah, well. Faint heart never won fair you know. How about it? I gotta eat, you gotta eat. Why not together?"

"Original, Lenn. Really original. But you're right. You ruined my evening. I see no reason why you shouldn't pay through the nose." She grabbed her purse. "I intend to order the most expensive meal on the menu. And," she tossed over her shoulder as she opened the door, "just a reminder, dinner's all that's on the agenda."

"Anything you say," Lenn said meekly as he followed her down the hall.

Too meekly, Katie thought.

Candles in little crystal chimneys dotted the room with flickering warmth. The soft clink of silverware and glasses gently underscored the mellow music of the suavely tuxedoed pianist at the shiny black baby grand in the center of the room. Potted palms and split-leaf philodendron discreetly separated tables set for two. The small restaurant reeked of romantic interlude.

Katie glared at Lenn.

He ignored her, and the second after the waiter took their drink order, he pulled his chair around the table and plunked it next to hers, justifying the move with, "I'm so used to seeing only your profile while we're cruising in the van that I'm uncomfortable looking at you straight on. Makes my eyes hurt."

She cast him a withering sidelong glance. "You could fertilize my mother's flower bed with that load."

"So okay, the truth is, I want to drool down your cleavage." Lenn leaned a little closer and eyed the front of the dress that Katie had told herself she'd put on for Dan. "What is it with you? You got something against romance?"

"No. But I do have something against being used in the name of romance."

"Used." He shot her a hard look. "That's a pretty strong word."

"Deny it then." Katie fingered the edge of the crisp white napkin before raising her eyes to meet Lenn's, which were altogether too near. "Look me straight in the eye and tell me you're not after my body."

"I'm not after your body."

She had to laugh. "Your nose is growing, Pinocchio. And your breath is melting my makeup. Back off a little."

"Come on, Katie. Let's stop playing games here." He slid an arm along the back of her chair. "I want you, and I intend to have you. Tonight."

"Oh, that's cute. Hold the thought, just don't hold your breath."

Lenn trailed a finger across the back of Katie's neckline. "What do I have to do to melt you, anyway? Light a Bunsen burner under your chair?"

Putting every effort into controlling the shiver that was creeping across her back, she leaned closer to the table, and farther away from Lenn. "That'd work a whole lot faster than the worn-out lines you've been trying."

The waiter interrupted with their drinks. Lenn sat back and lifted his glass to his lips, sipping the amber liquid pensively while he watched her over the rim. "You're not taking me seriously at all, are you?"

"Should I?"

"I think you know you should." His soft words sounded like a threat.

Only Lenn didn't frighten her anymore. He had a tender spot. She knew that now. She'd seen it. Meeting his narrowed gaze with a naughty grin, she taunted. "Ah, yes . . . I've heard about your lethal technique. Such a shame it isn't working at the moment."

"Look, Katie," he insisted. "Cutesy banter isn't going to work. Not tonight. We're going to spend a long, hot night together. You might as well reconcile yourself to that fact."

She was in trouble. She'd known it since Lenn had stood at her door with those darn flowers in his hand. He was right. She had been trying to hide behind a fast retort. And he was right, too, when he said it wasn't working. She had to find another angle. Yep, she was in trouble all right.

"Uh, Lenn, we're sort of partners, aren't we? At work, I mean?"

He took a long time answering. "Right. So?"

"So, you have to stop treating me like one of your harem. Look, I don't mean this in a bad way, but I know what kind of woman you're used to passing your time with, and I don't fit into that category. Quite simply, you're panting around the wrong fire hydrant. I don't go in for one-night stands."

"Don't tell me you believe all that crap?"

"Yes, I do. Now, if you could only see me as a friend—"

"A *friend!*" he choked. "You and me? Are you crazy?"

"Haven't you ever had a woman for a friend before? It can be quite rewarding, you know."

"Oh, come off it, Katie. Why are we even discussing this? You're being preposterous. It just isn't feasible."

"Why not?" The minute the words clattered out of her mouth, she knew she shouldn't have asked. The look in his eye said that he meant to prove why not.

Lenn reached onto the table and grabbed her hand, pulling it beneath the tablecloth and pressing it firmly into his lap. "That's *why not*. Got it? It's not possible."

Suppressing a gasp, she jerked her hand away, telling herself, *He wants to shock you. Don't let him.* She gritted out a smile. "Congratulations. I see nature didn't shortchange you, but we weren't talking physical endowments, we were discussing the possibility of becoming friends."

Lenn muttered a couple of words in graphic Italian. "Not *we*, lady. You. I want no part of this friends bit."

"Well, then." She rose calmly to her feet. "I guess it's time for me to leave, because anything beyond friendship is out of the question. I don't go to bed with men I don't know, and you don't let anyone get close enough to know you, so I guess we're at a stalemate. Breaking it is up to you, *friend*. Good night."

Lenn was dumbfounded as Katie spun on her dainty high heels and darted between tables toward the exit. She was outside before he snapped out of his paralysis, threw some cash on the table, and limped out after her. He caught up to her at the corner.

"Damn it, Katie. What's the idea of walking out like that?"

Aloofly, she glanced up at him. "It was pretty obvious to me that we were wasting each other's time, so I left."

"Well, it wasn't obvious to me."

"Yeah, well, that's the point. We're not on the same wave length. You're spaghetti, and I'm corned beef and cabbage. We just don't mix. Why don't you give up and save yourself the aggravation?"

Lenn slammed his hands onto his hips. "You're disrupting my whole life, do you know that?"

"No, Lenn." Katie was amazed. For once in her life, it was Lenn who was losing his cool while she was keeping hers. "You're doing that to yourself. I'm an innocent bystander."

"A bystander, maybe. Innocent, not likely. You have to have been around the block a few times to know how to tie a man into knots this way. You know damn well what you're doing to me."

Katie tapped a casual toe while she waited for the light to turn green, then marched across the street. On the other corner a hefty little man wearing a Dodger's cap was hawking hot dogs from a white-canopied cart. The aroma reminded her stomach how hungry it was.

Lenn grabbed her by the elbow. "Will you stop running? How can we have a decent fight if you keep dodging me?"

"You don't want a good fight. You want a good lay, and I'm not it. Sorry, pal."

A couple of people turned and gawked. Katie lowered her voice. "Find someone else. *I'm* not interested."

"Bull!" Ignoring their growing audience, Lenn didn't bother with a decrease in volume as he yelled in Katie's face, "I've seen the way you look at me when you think I'm not paying attention."

"Looking and touching are two different verbs. Look them up in the dictionary if you don't believe me."

The fat guy behind the hot dog cart put in his two cents' worth. "The lady's got a point, bud."

Lenn squinted at the man, then back at Katie. "I don't need a dictionary to tell me what's happening here. I want you. You want me. And I'm going to have you before this weekend's over, even if I have to tie you to a bed to do it."

"That's tellin' her, Rambo." The vendor grinned.

"Lower your voice," Katie hissed. "You're embarrassing me."

"I will not lower my voice." Lenn turned and shouted to all and sundry, "I intend to sleep with this woman by Sunday night. There!" He swiveled back to Katie. "Take that, you stubborn little broad."

"Why don't youse guys get married and get it over with? Then you can fight on your own turf," the hot dog man suggested.

Lenn dropped his head onto his chest. He took a long breath and set his lips in a thin line, then he turned to look down at the plump little vendor. "How much for a dog?"

The shorter man said, "Buck-fifty."

"I'll take one." Lenn toyed with the keys in his pocket until the hot dog was ready, then he slathered it with relish and onions, reached across the cart, opened the chubby vendor's mouth, and shoved the whole works inside, growling impatiently, "Maybe now you'll keep that trap shut. Now you . . ." He turned back to Katie, who couldn't help but laugh. "Are you going to come willingly or do I have to haul you off? Decide. Now. And stop that damned laughing."

By now, Katie wasn't the only one roaring. One man's belly laugh could be heard bellowing above the swelling titter of fascinated bystanders. This was probably the best entertainment they'd seen since the circus came to town. Katie tried to pull herself together, blurting out, "Lenn, this is crazy."

He didn't seem to agree. Catching her by the waist, he hoisted her a foot and a half off the sidewalk and pinned her against the building. She clutched at his shoulders for support, but she still couldn't stop laughing.

Then, he kissed her. Fiercely. And darned if her body didn't respond, even with half the population of L.A. looking on. Her merriment quickly subsided, and her heart started slamming wildly against her ribs. When Lenn released her, she sort of slid down the wall, not noticing, much less caring that the hem of her dress had rolled up. The only thing that really registered was that Lenn was staring into her eyes and lowering his mouth to hers again. He nibbled and tasted until she was limp with longing, then he bent and jounced her over his shoulder, limping down the street while the crowd cheered him on.

Lenn paced the living-room floor, keeping one eye on his unwilling captive, who was staring at him innocently from the sofa. What in heaven's name was he going to do with her? Every one of his instincts told him she wanted him as badly as he wanted her, and as far as women were concerned, his instincts were usually dead on. Why wouldn't she cooperate? He wasn't about to force her no matter what he'd spouted earlier, and damned if the smug little baggage didn't know that. But he wasn't about to let her off the hook, either. How would that look on his record? Besides, he'd already invested too much time and energy in her to just give up.

He stopped pacing and gave it one more shot. "What would it take to get you into my bed?"

"More than you're offering, that's for sure." Katie curled her hand into a loose fist and stared at her fingernails.

"Commitment? Is that it?"

"Lenn, this is pointless. All you want is a roll in the sack, and all I want is to be left alone. Find someone else. Go see Jenna."

"I don't want Jenna, I want you."

"No chance." Katie met his glare with a steady resolve.

Lenn turned away, wandered over to his favorite chair, and flung himself into it. He watched her over twined fingers.

Hell, he wasn't even aroused anymore. Hadn't been since he'd dumped her onto his couch. Yet he'd been stalking around the room trying to convince her to give in. He wondered if she realized what he'd really admitted when he told her he didn't want Jenna, that he wanted her. Even *he* had been shaken at the uncomfortable realization that no other woman would do.

He needed to face some home truths. How long could he hold out for this woman? And would she be worth it? What if she'd said yes a few minutes ago, when he'd asked if she wanted commitment? Would he have walked away?

An answer came back, mocking, resounding in his head. No.

He bolted out of his chair. "That's it, Katie. You win. I'm taking you home."

NINE

Katie hid in the darkroom all morning and part of
the afternoon, grateful that the phone hadn't rung to
summon her out on a story. Around three, she called
herself a coward and marched up to the newsroom
and over to her desk. Ignoring the man slumped at
the VDT beside her, she plunked into her chair,
pulled a few lenses out of her case, and started polishing them.

Lenn stood up abruptly and walked to the back of
the newsroom to read the printout coming in on the
wire service.

So much for ignoring him. He evidently intended
to beat her to the punch. She peeked over her camera
case. The light-blue cotton shirt he wore stretched
tight across his hunched back, defining each rippling
muscle. She willed her fingers to rub the soft cloth
across the lens when they really wanted to stroke the
man across the room. Her body was as traitorous this
morning as it had been last night.

Last night she'd been about two seconds away from throwing all that caution she'd been hoarding to the wind and giving in to what she admitted to herself she wanted. Lenn. Only he had chosen that moment to bolt out of his chair as if his pants were on fire. She still wondered what had shaken him so thoroughly. Would she ever figure out what made him tick? He was like a chameleon, changing the very second a person got used to the skin he was wearing.

Katie tried to focus on the job at hand, cleaning lenses that were already spotless, but her eyes acted on their own and kept returning to the man who, to all appearances, was intent on the news happening around the world. Suddenly, she saw him stiffen and lean forward. Good, it looked like a story was coming in. It was about time. She was about to pack away her lenses when Lenn turned. He was as white as the immaculate sheets that used to hang on her grandmother's clothesline. Stiff and unseeing, he moved past her and out of the newsroom door.

Katie looked back at the other reporter who'd been standing near Lenn. Her eyes signaled a silent question that was answered with a puzzled shrug of his shoulders.

Propelling out of her chair, she ran into the hall after Lenn, only to see the elevator door jerk closed on his back. She raced for the stairs, leaping down three at a time.

She hadn't stopped to see what had prompted his reaction, but she knew it wasn't just a story. Something had gotten to him. Pain had been etched in every line of his body.

He needed her.

Lenn was slumped over the steering wheel of his car when Katie yanked open the passenger door and clambered inside. "Lenn . . ."

"Get out, Katie." The low growl didn't even sound like Lenn.

"Lenn, I—"

He looked up then, his face contorted with an emotion Katie couldn't even begin to read.

"I said, get out. I don't want you here."

"I'm not leaving." *You need me*, she cried silently, instinctively knowing he wouldn't want to hear the words.

"Damn it, Katie, I said, get out."

"No."

His eyes narrowed in torment and anger, and for a minute she thought his rage would erupt and that he would throw her from the car. When he didn't, she recognized that he was in too much pain to make the effort.

"It's on your own head then." He ground the key in the ignition and peeled out of the parking lot, flinging Katie against the door as he slashed around the corner. She scrambled to fasten her seat belt, then held onto the armrest for dear life.

Lenn drove like a man possessed, and Katie was astounded that he wasn't stopped by an army of police as he ran more than one red light before he hit the freeway. The speedometer hit one hundred, then one-ten. Katie swallowed but didn't say a word. She couldn't. They were all stuck somewhere down in her chest.

A terror-filled eternity later, he came to a careening stop at the end of a dirt road leading to a deserted beach. They were obviously on private property, but

Lenn didn't look like he gave a damn about the law of trespass.

"Lenn . . . I—"

"Shut up, Katie. I don't want you here, so just shut up." He flung open the car door and shot out of his seat. Katie reached for the handle of her door, but a dead voice stopped her cold. "I don't want you with me."

Katie slumped in her seat and watched Lenn walk onto the beach. He stood staring at the water, and Katie sat staring at Lenn. She gave him an hour before she quietly got out of the Corvette and joined him.

"What happened, Lenn?"

He whipped around at the soft sound of her voice, his brow furled as if he'd forgotten she was there. The pain in his eyes hadn't seemed to have diminished, and for a minute she thought he'd tell her to leave again.

He turned back to the water, and stooping to pick up a small piece of driftwood, he flung it far into the gently lapping ocean. "A couple of reporters were found at the edge of a jungle down in Nicaragua. Their hands and feet were bound, and they each had a bullet in their brains."

Lenn hooked his hands in his back pockets and moved farther down the beach. Katie sucked in a long breath of sea air and followed. "And?"

"And nothing."

Nothing, her foot. Horrible news items came over the wire daily, and Lenn viewed them with the detachment she'd learned a reporter had to have if he expected to survive in the world of journalism. There had to be something personal involved this time.

"Did you know them?"

"No."

Okay, that left—what? Something from the time he'd been there. This had to have something to do with whatever happened that he'd been so damned close-mouthed about. And it was gnawing at him. She had to make him spit it out—for his own stubborn sake. Only she needed to find the key. What could it be? Think. What had he told her?

Not too much. Only that he'd gone there to see what happened to a friend. A friend who happened to be a reporter. What was his name? She closed her eyes and searched through her memory.

"Tell me about Enrico."

Lenn stopped so suddenly that Katie nearly slammed into his back. Bingo, she thought. He turned and skewered her with a dark, angry glare. "Damn it, Katie, don't you ever give up?"

"Not when it really counts. Look at you. Whatever's bothering you is eating at you. You need to talk about it. That's the only way you're ever going to get rid of it."

"Did you ever think that maybe I don't want to get rid of it?"

"That's stupid, Lenn."

"No, what's stupid is butting into something that doesn't concern you. But then, that's what this is all about, isn't it? You never could leave well enough alone. Heaven forbid that there should be something that nosy little Katie O'Brien doesn't know."

"Lenn, it isn't like that. I—"

"Isn't it? You've been on my back ever since I was dumb enough to mention I was ever in Nicaragua. Well, lady, you've asked one time too many."

Lenn's eyes flashed with a heated fury that frightened her. A violent, surging fury that encroached on the tiny space between them. Instinctively, she backed away.

"Oh, no, Katie, you asked for it." Lenn grabbed her arms, forcing her to face his desperate pain. "You wanted to hear all about Enrico. You're going to listen to every pretty word."

Self-preservation almost made her pull away from the hard bite of the fingers that were digging holes in the tender flesh of her arms, but she bore the hurt, more than willing to take the brunt of his welling rage.

"It took months. Months of slogging through dense jungles following rumor after rumor. When I found him, he was tied to a chair in an abandoned shack with a soldier towering over him, jabbing him in the gut with the butt of a rifle. I didn't even stop to think. I grabbed a rock, crept inside, and cracked the guard on the head. When I untied Enrico, he could barely stand, but I was puffed up with some damned hero complex." He gave a derisive snort. "So I hauled him upright and half dragged, half pushed him across the clearing to where we'd hidden the jeep. We were nearly there when the firing started. I felt him slump in my arms. They got him right between the eyes. He was dead before he hit the ground." Lenn tightened his hold, and Katie had to bite her lip to keep from crying out. "Is that enough for you, or do you want me to tell you how his eyes stared without seeing, or how his brains were splattered halfway across the clearing?"

He wrenched his hands from her arms so violently that she had to stumble to retain her balance, and with an agonized groan, he spun away and lunged blindly down the beach. Katie let him go, her hand covering her mouth, her insides twisted in an aching knot. She wanted to shout, "I'm sorry," but she held back the words she knew were useless. Inadequate.

She watched until he disappeared behind an outcropping of rock then crumpled to the sand. And cried.

When the tears dried, she gave an inelegant sniff, and wiping her face on the sleeve of her shirt, stood and dusted off the clinging sand, before starting down the beach in the direction Lenn had taken.

She found him sitting amid a small pile of rocks, his head cradled in his hands. Silently, she perched on a large boulder about five feet away. Time, uncaring, ticked on, and Katie waited.

"You were right." Lenn spoke quietly, finally dropping his hands and turning in her direction. The anger had abated in the dark recesses of his eyes but a quiet hint of torment remained. "It did help to spit it out," he clarified with a tiny, wry tilt at the corner of his mouth. "Aren't you going to say, I told you so?"

"Nah, I never state the obvious." Katie focused on a lone windsurfer cutting across the waves. God, it hurt to keep it light.

She let minutes slip past before she succumbed to her all-encompassing need to know and asked, "How did you get away?"

His only hesitation was a deep, fortifying breath. "The villagers who were helping me managed to kill the other two soldiers who'd materialized out of the jungle. But it was too late for Enrico. God, the whole thing was so futile."

Lenn, too, stared out at the bright yellow-and-red sail scudding along the horizon, and as if a dam had finally been opened, he began to talk. Horrors of a war that no one ever won spilled forth into the soft, cooling wind that had begun to blow in off the darkening water. Katie listened, long past wanting to hear, simply because he needed to tell, and when he was spent, he stood and held out an arm. Without a word, she rose and curled into the welcoming space beneath his shoulder, and they walked silently back up the beach.

The hot sun had lowered its heavy, shimmering mass to tease at the rippling surface of the glittering ocean. Lingering, they watched as the flattening disc melted into the deep green water. And in the warm glow of twilight, Lenn turned her toward him. She slid her free arm to meet the other behind his waist. A playful breeze lifted a curling strand of hair and flipped it across her mouth. With the gentlest of touches, Lenn brushed the errant tendril from her lips.

"Oh, God, Katie," he rasped as his mouth covered hers, devouring the very essence of her as though he were a man coming off a month-long hunger strike. He sipped and savored every taste, and Katie was consumed as surely as the sea had swallowed the fire of the sun. When the need for air forced them apart, Lenn lowered his forehead to hers and dragged in a replenishing breath. "You sure do pick your times to get all soft and compliant."

"Lenn, I . . ."

"Shh." He held a finger to her lips, then caressed their swollen fullness with his thumb. "Just, shh."

A jogger thudded past them, casting a curious look

in their direction. Lenn tucked her back beneath his arm and headed to where they had left the car. "You hungry? I think somewhere along the way we missed dinner."

Katie nodded, though she was too full of conflicting emotion to allow room for something so prosaic as food.

"Good, I make a mean omelet."

Katie leaned her elbows on the table and propped her head onto curled fists and sighed. She was surprisingly, satisfyingly sated.

"Was I right or what?" Lenn poked out the tip of his tongue to catch a tiny dab of egg at the corner of his quirking lips.

Katie swallowed hard. God, how she loved that man, wanted him. She dropped her hands to the edge of the table and shoved. No, she hadn't thought what she thought she thought. She couldn't. Picking up her plate, she ignored Lenn's puzzled curl of eyebrows as she carried it to the sink. Not Lenn. Not the Lenn she'd spent half her life despising.

"Well?"

"Well, what?" She wouldn't look at him. That's what it was, he was distracting her with all that Italian charm and good looks.

"Do I make a mean omelet?"

"Oh, yeah, I guess you do."

"Just guess?"

"Okay, okay, you make a mean omelet." Why didn't he shut up. She had to think this thing through. Out of the corner of one eye, she watched as he scraped the leavings on his plate into the trash can. His shirt pulled tightly across the muscles of his back. Every stupid shirt he owned had the nasty habit of doing that. Lord, she wanted him. She closed her eyes and leaned against the sink. If he appealed to her when he was scraping garbage, she must love him, but, damn it, she didn't want to.

He had touched her today, not because he had told her such a horror of a story, but because he had finally opened up a deeper part of himself. He had shown her a piece of him that ached, that cared, and that sharing had invited caring in return. And she, soft-headed fool she'd always been, had gone overboard, as usual, and fallen in love. The only trouble was that it wasn't going to change things one iota. Lenn might have given her a glimpse of another side of him, but the part of him she couldn't handle hadn't changed. He was still a man who would never commit, and it didn't help one bit that she now had an inkling of why.

Lenn's voice penetrated her thoughts. "Ever been to Cardiff-by-the-Sea?"

"Sorry, what?"

"Cardiff-by-the-Sea, down near San Diego. Ever been there?"

"Uh, no. Why?" Katie set a soapy plate she hadn't even noticed she'd been washing onto the drainer for Lenn to dry.

"I'm driving down for the weekend to get in a little surfing. Wanna come?"

She heard herself breathe, "Yeah, I think I'd like that," then cursed herself for being a total and complete idiot. "I don't surf, but I could watch."

"You'll surf."

"Lenn," she groaned, exasperated that she could

love a man who was so darn bossy. "I just told you I don't know how."

"I'll teach you."

"Uh, I don't know about that."

"What's the matter? Don't you trust me?" He spotted the raising of her eyebrows. "Never mind. Forget I asked."

Only that was the trouble. She couldn't forget, because the bottom line was that she *didn't* trust him—at least not with her heart.

"Hey, I didn't dump you off the dirt bike, and I didn't let you fall out of the chopper. I think I can manage to keep you on a surfboard."

"Okay, okay, I'll give it a shot."

She had to smile as he outlined the weekend's plans with the same kind of enthusiasm he put into everything he did.

"You really do love your life, don't you? Just taking off someplace, whenever the mood strikes you?" she asked, not really wanting to hear the answer.

"Yeah, I do. What about you? You happy with yours?"

"Most times. I'm close to my family. I guess that helps."

Lenn nodded ruefully, "Yes, I imagine it would."

"You imagine?"

"Well, I'm not really all that close to mine," he shrugged. "But then, maybe that's partly my fault."

"What do you mean?" Katie finished wiping the counter and turned to lean against it.

"Well, first there's Mom, trying to marry me off every time I show my face. Then there's Sal, who keeps hinting that he intends to leave the paper in my hands when he's ready to retire. It's a pain. I love them, but they keep pushing. And the harder they push, the faster I run.''

Wasn't that the truth? Katie hated herself, but she had to ask, ''And is Jenna your mom's latest prospect?''

Lenn nodded with a disgusted huff.

''She's very . . . attractive.''

''I suppose, but she's so damned domestic she terrifies me.''

The way he twisted his face into a disgusted grimace made her chuckle. ''You have something against domesticity?''

''With Jenna? You better believe it.'' He raised his voice to a high, nagging pitch. ''Where ya goin', Lenny? What time you comin' home, Lenny? Did ya take out the garbage, Lenny?'' he shook his head. ''No, Katie, that's not for me.''

''Well, I can't say I blame you, but . . .''

''Would you be like that?''

The question threw her for a loop. She stared at him wide-eyed and open-lipped.

''Well, would you?'' he repeated.

''I would hope not.''

''So would I.'' He reached over, took her hand, and pulled her into the living room. Parking himself on the floor with his back leaning against the couch, he pushed the coffee table out of the way with his foot and patted the carpet in front of him. She hesitated only a second before sitting down between his legs and leaning her back against his chest. As naturally as if they had sat that way a thousand times before, his arms went around her and she tilted her head against his shoulder.

Sometime during the long afternoon of revelations, the quarreling had stopped and the hugging had begun. The transition had occurred so smoothly and so naturally that it was difficult to imagine being any other way. Lenn's hand slid up her arm, over her shoulder, and closed around the column of her neck, stroking her with a slow gentleness that sent an electric tingle through every one of her nerve endings, causing her blood to course through her veins like red-hot lava. She shivered. Her reaction was far too strong for such a simple touch, and she was forced to recognize that it wouldn't be long before she tossed her doubts to the wildest wind and took what pleasure his touch promised.

Though her tremor had been slight, he felt it and inquired softly, "What's wrong?"

"Nothing. I just got a chill." *Oh, brilliant, Katie. It must be ninety degrees in here, for heaven's sake.* She could feel him smiling against her hair. His hand, the one around her neck, slipped under the collar of her blouse and settled in a full-size spread slightly above her cleavage. With a slow up-and-down motion, his finger fanned down to explore the valley between her breasts. It was as if he was testing the waters before jumping in.

From where she sat she could see two options. One: she could get out of there while the getting was good. Or two: she could respond the way he so obviously wanted. The latter was the easier choice by far, until she had to face herself in the morning. She steeled herself to show no reaction, but had to wonder if he could feel her heart thumping beneath his hand. A long, charged moment later, his hand shifted down, stilling on the swell of her breasts just above the white lace of her delicate nothing of a bra.

She shuddered again and he whispered, "Stay with me tonight."

Of course she wouldn't. She couldn't. It was entirely out of the question. She opened her mouth to tell him and somehow the words came out, "I don't have my makeup bag."

"You don't need it," he spoke softly into her ear. "Your kind of beauty shines from within. Tell me you'll stay. Please?"

Brushing her hair aside, he burnt a trail of hot, searing kisses along the side of her neck, nibbling, tasting, then catching the lobe of her ear between his lips and sucking on it slowly. Persuasively. Too damned persuasively. The long, lean legs that hugged her body on either side were too persuasive. The natural, masculine scent of him was too persuasive. Everything about him was just too persuasive to allow her to think.

He waited for an answer, but torn by indecision, she couldn't give him one. She found it physically impossible to force a *no* through her parted lips. Slowly, he dragged his hand out of her blouse and nudged her forward. Placing his hands around her waist, he urged her to stand, then followed her up. He slid his arm around her waist as if he knew how wobbly her legs had suddenly become and led her gently around the corner toward his bedroom.

She stopped at the door and gazed up into his desire-darkened eyes. "I'm not sure about this, Lenn."

His slow smile was patient. "You've come this far. Just a few steps more and we're home."

Home was a king-size bed with a wild gray animal skin spread across a black satin bedspread. Plants were everywhere, long leafy plants, hanging low over the bed creating a junglelike setting. The room was untamed and strange, with an uninhibited kind of allure. Like the man who slept there. Above the bed, in a glass cabinet, was a collection of ancient knives with ivory and abalone handles. Katie stared at them and swallowed. Hard.

"So . . . this is home, eh?" She swallowed again. Nerves had always made her mouth dry, and right now it felt as if she had swallowed the Sahara Desert.

Lenn cupped her face in his hand, teasing her mouth with a much too brief kiss. "Yeah, this is it. What do you think?"

Think? Who could think? "It's . . . primitive. Definitely you." She cast an anxious eye around the lush, sultry room.

"Second thoughts?" Lenn brushed the pad of his thumb across her trembling lower lip.

"Third and fourth. Maybe tenth?" Her tongue darted out to wet her lips and tangled with his thumb, tasting, against her will, the hot, addictive salt of his skin.

"It'll be good between us."

She lifted her gaze to meet the simmering passion reflected in his and knew he was only stating a truth.

"I know," she whispered.

She was going to be hurt. That much was a certainty. Lenn would one day walk away from her, to another adventure or, even more painfully, to another woman. She'd been warned too often not to believe that. Not only by her brother, but by Lenn himself. Tonight, though still self-protective enough to hesitate, she was ready to take whatever Lenn was willing to give. She loved him, and although she had never been one for easy platitudes, somewhere in the back of what remained of her conscious mind, she knew that a short-lived moment of love was infinitely more preferable than an empty void with no love at all.

The back of Lenn's fingertips teased along her breasts as he slowly undid the buttons of her blouse. Tiny, stinging shocks trailed after them. She couldn't help but wonder how it was going to feel when he really touched her. Time seemed to slow, and she felt the collar of her shirt slip off her shoulders, and in the dreamlike stillness, she watched it fold to the floor. Piece by piece, he removed her clothing until she stood before him, naked as the day she was born.

"You're everything I imagined." Lenn traced a sizzling line from the throbbing pulse at the side of her neck down to the valley between her breasts. "Every delicious, freckled inch of you."

Katie licked at her lips. "You always made fun of my freckles. I hated them."

"Just shows you how stupid I was. Tonight, I plan to spend a long night tasting every sweet one." He led her to the side of the bed and gently pressed her onto the soft, sensual fur, bending to make good his promise as the tip of his tongue darted to savor a small dot of pigment on the inner side of her left breast. She nearly cried out in agony when he straightened to remove his own clothes. Avidly, she watched while he uncovered that wonderful golden expanse of chest and the long sinewy corded muscles of his thighs, which were marred only by the long dark slash still stitched with black thread. She raised onto an elbow and reached to stroke the still-reddened injury. "Oh, Lenn."

"It's okay. It doesn't hurt much anymore. I intend to take it slow and easy anyway." He lifted her hand from his thigh and kissed the tip of each finger before releasing her to hook his own fingers into the waistband of his skimpy white briefs. The scrap of material slid down his slim hips and released his manhood from bondage. He was enjoying her eager perusal as he stood before her proud and erect, a testimony to how badly he wanted her.

When he finally joined her on the bed she was ready to scream with need.

Leaning on one strong elbow, he circled the peaking nipple of her breast. "I've dreamed about this, you know."

"So have I," she admitted.

"You afraid?"

"Yeah."

"So am I."

His kisses were tender and all-encompassing, setting every inch of her skin aflame. His hands grazed a slow journey along her burning flesh, and she felt as if she had become weightless and was floating off into some beauteous, surrealistic cosmos from which she never wanted to return. Her love swelled, yet for all the exquisite ecstasy he was showing her now— even now—she remembered that her moments with him were not timeless. He would be gone when the loving was over. Just thinking about it caused a desperation to well up deep within her. She clung to his shoulders and arched her back to receive his marauding mouth, and a warm tear trickled into her hairline.

Waking up beside Lenn Domina wasn't something Katie had prepared herself for, mainly because she never would have imagined that such an event was possible. Yet instead of worrying about the misgivings she knew were sure to come, she lay quietly and savored the moment, letting her eyes travel down the length of his magnificent body. The black satin bedspread draped him as if he were a baroque statue carved in Italian marble and the sleek, silken folds delineated every taut, well-developed muscle. Oh, how she was tempted to run a hand along—

"Morning."

Katie started at the sound of the husky, sleep-warmed voice. Her instinctive self-preservation mechanism kicked in, and she clutched the sheet tightly under her arms, suddenly too aware that she was as naked as the body she'd been caught so blatantly admiring. "Um, good morning."

She avoided looking into his eyes, but she knew

he was examining her intently, more intently than she was ready to deal with yet. A warm flush infused her pores and she just knew that her skin was blending with the color of her hair.

"Morning-after jitters?" he guessed, altogether too accurately.

"Yeah, I guess I'm not as used to this sort of thing as you are." And that was probably the true source of her anxiety, if she was going to be honest about the whole thing.

"Katie?" He hooked a forefinger under her chin and turned her to face him. He looked as uncertain as she felt. "Look, I'm having a little trouble sorting this out myself, but one thing I do know is that whatever happened here isn't like . . . well, it isn't a casual thing. I want you to know that, all right?"

Katie nodded, but she wasn't at all certain she believed him. He'd dumped a lot of pain yesterday and maybe all that had happened between them had been a residue reaction. A physical release of frustration. But she didn't want it to be that. She wanted to believe him.

He read the expressions that must have been flitting across her face and saw her doubts. "I wasn't using you," he echoed the words she had flung at him so many times in the last couple of weeks. "If you don't believe anything else, at least believe that." He slid out of bed and, totally unconscious of his nudity, strolled to a bureau, took out a pair of dark navy briefs, and slipped them on.

He turned toward her just before he moved out the door. "Stay where you are." The words were a plea, not the order they sounded, and they both were all too cognizant of the fact. "I'll see what I can scrounge up for breakfast. Be right back."

She resisted the urge to bolt. Scuttling back to lean against the headboard, she tried instead to make sense of her feelings. The loving had been good. No, it had been darn near perfect, reaching far above and beyond her expectations. Lenn had introduced her to passions within herself she hadn't even known existed, and if he were anyone but who he was, she would have had no trouble believing in what had happened between them. But as it was, she had a hard time getting around all her ingrained childhood mistrust, especially since it had been augmented by years of listening to rumors about Lenn's exploits with the ladies. All that emotional baggage had merely left her feeling more confused than ever.

And she was nowhere near sorting out that confusion when Lenn reappeared carrying a tray that held a box of Ritz crackers, a jar of Cheez Whiz, and two cans of Coke. He slid the tray onto her knees and crawled in beside her.

"Breakfast?" She couldn't help herself. She laughed. Grabbing a cracker from the box, she slathered it with cheese and popped it into her mouth as Lenn opened the pop, swearing when the metal tab snapped off the second can.

"Yeah, well, gourmet isn't my thing this early in the morning." He struggled to shove the rest of the tab through the lid of the can, smugly exclaiming, "Gotcha, you little sucker," when he finally succeeded.

Suddenly, Katie felt good. She didn't care. Sorting out things wasn't important. What was important was that she was with Lenn, irrepressibly, delightfully funny Lenn. The man she loved.

He took a long slug of Coke. "So how are you feeling, anyway?"

"Satisfied," she answered softly, shifting her slightly embarrassed gaze to the cracker box on the tray.

"Good." He reached into the box. "The feeling's mutual."

"Really?"

"Couldn't you tell?"

"Yeah, well, I don't really have anything substantial to compare it to." She thought about Brian and Dan. No, she sure didn't.

"I'm glad." He dipped a knife into the jar. "Take my word for it. You're looking at one satisfied man."

"Well, now that you've had your way, at least you won't be hounding me anymore." She tried to sound unconcerned, looking at her lap so her eyes couldn't give her away.

Lenn had a cracker halfway to his mouth and stopped to stare at her unbelievingly. "That isn't what you want, is it? For me to leave you alone?"

Pride made her answer, "I didn't really expect anything else."

"And what if that's not what I want? Then what?"

"Then I don't know. I never considered the possibility you'd want it any other way." Which was the hundred-percent truth.

"Well, start considering it. Start soon." He tossed the cracker into his mouth and crunched it whole.

Katie felt her heart skip a beat, maybe two. She turned to look at him. "C'mon, Lenn, don't start saying things you don't mean. I'm a big girl. I can take a little—"

"Damn it, Katie. I'm telling you I *want* you to expect something from me. This is new to me, too. I know I'm asking an awful lot, but take a chance on me. Trust me a little."

Oh, God, how she wanted to. "And while I'm taking a chance on you, what will you be doing? It works both ways, you know."

Lenn reached across and lifted the tray from her lap and set it on the floor beside the bed. Curling his hands around her shoulders, he turned her to face him. His reply was simple; his eyes, trusting. "I'm taking a chance just by telling you these things. Don't you know that by now?"

She buried her face in his neck, her insides quivering with pent-up emotion. "God help me, Lenn, but I think I will take that chance."

Everything was forgotten in that moment. All her doubts, her fears, her misgivings; everything was forgotten. Everything but the feel of his warm body moving toward her under the blanket.

Cardiff-by-the-Sea was paradise on earth. The town itself was spread out along a crest that was curved like a half moon to surround the beach below. From the shore, one could barely see the tops of buildings on the high horizon, muted pastel etchings against a hazy white sky.

The highway divided the scene in half. Trees, shrubs, and ferns of varying hues of green, yellow, orange, and brown colored the rock-strewn slope below the town, gradually thinning, and thinning still, until only a twig sprouted here and there along the sand crowding one side of the highway. On the other side of the winding stretch of road was Cardiff Beach and a sprawling three-unit motel that once had been a Spanish casa but was now a resting place, a watering hole, a peaceful hideaway for those wanting to get away from it all.

Few people from the town ever went to the beach, possibly because it was a thing taken for granted since it was always there. But for a handful of beautiful brown surfers migrating to catch the almighty wave, it was a summer home. Colorful vans were set up like a Gypsy camp, and the sand was dotted with lawn chairs, surfboards, and makeshift barbecues, which were lit only when the sun went down. And when the sun went down over Cardiff, it was a thing to behold. A beauty that defied description. A grand photodrama directed by the hand of the Ultimate Artist.

The motel was vacant except for the manager, an old Ukrainian woman named Nadia who made a few extra dollars reading tarot cards when business was slow. Lenn and Katie chose the largest unit. It had a large white kitchen with red-and-white tiles that were buffed to a high sheen. Heavy cedar beams stretched across the high ceilings and the living-room floors were polished hardwood, setting off the large gray-and-white bear rug that sprawled in front of the old stone fireplace. Though the furniture was dated, it was in mint condition. The sofa was a cozy deep royal-blue velvet and the tables, natural wood.

While Katie unpacked, Lenn took a long hike into town for some groceries. Hanging his shirts and jeans on one side of the closet and her own things on the other, she felt as if she were playing house. She smiled at herself for sniffing each item of his clothing before hooking them onto hangers. When she was done, she went for a stroll down the beach with a bag of tortilla chips to feed the sea gulls. Loping along the sand, she waved the bag in one hand and tossed chips into the air with the other. The soft summer breeze blew through her hair, and she laughed.

Yet beneath the laughter, her soul was leaden with melancholy. Every moment she spent with Lenn was so precious, even more so because of the fear that each might be the last. She stored every second in her heart for that inevitable, rainy day when he would stop wanting her.

Why did she have to love him? She hadn't planned it. Hadn't sought it. Didn't want it, in fact. But she was stuck with it, and she had never known such happiness or such agony in all her life. The two conflicting emotions melded somehow, intensifying each other to the point of drawing tears straight up from her soul. Folding down onto the sand, she set the chips aside and drew her knees close to her chest and stared out at the ocean.

A half hour later, she rose and scuffed along the beach back to the motel, leaving the bag of chips where they lay in the sand. She wandered through the back door at the same time Lenn came whistling in through the front. Across the wide expanse of the living room, he pulled a bottle from the grocery bag and tossed it at her.

"Here, have a Gatorade. It'll put hair on your chest."

She snatched the bottle out of the air. "No thanks. Electrolysis is too expensive these days." She dropped the drink back into the bag as he passed her on the way to the kitchen.

"Hey, what's a little hair," he teased. "My aunt Luch's got a full beard and we love her anyway."

Katie smiled in spite of herself. Impulsively, she threw her arms around his neck, crunching the bag of food between them. "You fool. What am I going to do with you?"

Lenn slid the bag from between them, set it on the counter, and drew her close. "You, sweet thing, can do anything you want with me."

"Oh, Lenn . . ." she sighed, "what will I do after you've moved on."

"Don't do this to yourself, Katie." He planted a kiss on her nose and turned to unpack the groceries. "You're assuming that our days together are numbered. That kind of thinking can really screw up a relationship as new as ours. Let's take it one day at a time. Enjoy what we have together." He glanced over his shoulder. "Okay?"

She stifled another sigh. Columbus was wrong, she decided. There *was* an edge to the earth, and she was falling over it as surely as her name was Katie O'Brien.

He tossed the last bag of Oreos into the cupboard. "It's a great day out there. How 'bout a little surfing?"

She wasn't exactly in the mood for anything that required any kind of concentration since hers was now shattered, but she was here with him, so she figured she might as well make the most of it. "I suppose," she mumbled without much enthusiasm. "You sure you're ready to surf with that bum leg?"

"I made out fine with it last night," he grinned. "Pun intended."

Katie groaned and headed for the bedroom to change into her swimsuit. He wouldn't give in to physical pain no matter now intense it got. Sometimes the man could be as tough as old folks' toenails.

For all his cocky bravado, after three nosedives into the powerful, white water—the plunges resulting from trying to keep Katie on the surfboard—Lenn had to admit, however silently, that the ache in his leg wouldn't let him go on. Alone, he was certain he'd have no problem conquering the waves, pain or not, but Katie was a damn sight far from being graceful on the water. Though, he had to note, her breasts had a certain buoyancy that encouraged forgiveness for her ineptitude.

A silent agreement to give up surfing for the day was finalized with a nod when Katie gazed wistfully at the shore. It was pretty obvious she wasn't exactly enjoying herself.

Lenn grabbed the board and followed her as she waded toward the sand, his eyes glued to her shimmery, wet backside where the lightweight white spandex clung to her curves. He reveled in the slight jiggling of feminine flesh, and he wanted her again. Here. Now. Forget foreplay, even. He craved immediate satisfaction. Hot, intense, grinding . . .

"Go sit down for a while," she commanded softly. "You're limping again."

Lenn jammed the surfboard into the sand. "I'd rather *lie* down. With you. Alone."

Her eyes locked with his. In the direct afternoon

sunlight her eyes were so clear and so green they took his breath away. He was rocked by the unexpected swell of feeling that seemed to have risen from the ocean's depths. Her pure gold lashes glistened in the sun, inspiring sheer enchantment in his soul, and the levity he'd felt only seconds ago was swallowed up as surely as the waves from the Pacific had followed them up the sand and erased their footsteps. The moment stretched warm and deep and endless.

When was the last time that time itself had stood still for him? he wondered. When was the last time passion had sat in the rumble seat while another emotion, ten times more intoxicating, moved up front to steer the way?

The answers came in the form of memories. Crystal-clear flashbacks of another time and place—yes, even another life that was infinitely distant, and yet painfully close. Suzanna. Suzanna, whose laughter never lost its lovely musical sound in spite of the hateful, ugly explosions of war all around them. Sweet, gentle Suzanna. Strong Suzanna.

The eyes he gazed into were not brown, nor was the hair gleaming sable, but he knew, suddenly and so very certainly, that their owner possessed that same combination of softness and strength that was, for him, so vital in a woman, though so few possessed it anymore.

He had walked through hell with an angel, and, ironically, he was the one who had survived. Now, the time had come to reflect upon that hell and come to terms with it. And who should be here to hold his hand but another angel. A fierce tremor sliced through his heart like a bolt of hot, searing lightning, and he acknowledged in this moment that he loved Katie O'Brien. She wasn't Suzanna, gentle or sweet. In fact, she was sometimes downright sassy and tart, but she gave of herself with the same honest caring that twined around him like wool around a spindle, binding him to her as surely as he had been tied once before.

There was no turning back. He was in as deep as a man could get—sinking like a body in quicksand, and all the reaching and struggling in the world wouldn't pull him back out.

"Hey, you going to lie down and let me put some lotion on that gorgeous back, or what?" Katie asked a little too brightly, valiantly trying to break into the reverie he knew she didn't understand. He dropped onto the towel they'd spread earlier and let her hands slide over his heated skin as he stared out at the water.

Heaven help me.

The fiery sunset gradually extinguished its flames in the cool amethyst waters of the darkening horizon. Spectacular, motley shades of hot and cold bled across the sky until darkness settled over the earth. Like exquisitely cut diamonds, thousands of dazzling, silvery stars shimmered in the velvet indigo dome that remained. And the moon—the moon was so bright and full, it looked as if it might burst.

Katie and Lenn sat side by side on an old blanket they had found on a high closet shelf. Hugging their knees, they sipped red Cabernet from weightless Styrofoam cups, each lost in thought yet distantly aware of white water slapping against hard rock and soft sand. Katie gazed out at the moon-glittered water and thought she'd give anything to know what was on Lenn's mind right then. He was unusually quiet— had been since this afternoon on the beach.

Silence was not always golden, she was beginning to discover. Sometimes it was black and insidious, eating at you and eroding fragile feelings that barely had time to solidify. Did his withdrawal mean he was tiring of her already, that he was regretting bringing her with him?

Lenn raised his cup to his lips, lightly brushing his arm against hers. She shivered and wondered how such a simple, innocent grazing of body hairs could affect her so strongly. Her gaze shifted from the hypnotic swell of the waves to lock with his. Her breath caught. His eyes could stir the seven seas, could fill her soul with emotions she couldn't begin to describe. He was so close she could smell the wine still damp on his lips. She remembered what magic those lips could perform and was momentarily distracted from trying to read the emotions in those coffee-brown eyes. His mouth tightened, then parted. Was he going to speak, to use that sometimes scalding brand of honesty he possessed? Or was he going to kiss her? She held her breath and waited.

Lenn shook his head, smiled thinly, and looked down at his cup. The moment shattered. He had left her hanging in suspense at the end of an emotional rope that was threatening to snap.

Damn him! Katie cursed him silently for the control he had over her moods, over her life, and turned to stare out at the dark water. He was twisting her inside out, and he didn't even know he was doing it. How could he know of the torment he had caused to rage inside her? How could she possibly tell him?

She couldn't. He was, quite unintentionally, killing her.

"There's something you should know about." Lenn drained the last dribble of wine in his cup.

Katie swallowed, aching, wondering if she should be glad he was finally going to talk or if she was about to be torn apart by what he was going to say.

"Whenever you asked me about Nicaragua, I kept putting you off—at least until the other day. Talking about it wasn't easy, and the rest of it's going to be even harder, so bear with me if I stumble all over myself . . ." Lenn's voice trailed off as he massaged his forehead pensively for a moment. "Enrico was only part of it. The other part . . . was Suzanna. She was a nurse in the village I used as my base while I looked for Enrico. She was one of the kindest, most unselfish human beings I've ever known. Amid all the corruption and cold-blooded murder going on around her, she still found room in her heart and in her home for anyone who needed it. She literally dragged the wounded home: men, women, children, Contras, Sandinistas. Who or what didn't matter to her. She believed everyone had the right to live. I fell in love with her. How could I not? We were married in an old shell of a church." Lenn paused, lost in memories.

Katie wanted to get up and run. Fast and far down the beach to where all the people were. She didn't want to hear any more, yet she needed to know it all. She stared down at the red liquid in her cup and listened.

"Sometimes she would go with me to search for Enrico, but when she discovered she was pregnant that stopped. Anyway, it seemed as if there was always someone to look after. God, she had such a capacity for giving, that lady. One day, November third—I'll never forget the date—I went out as usual, and when it started to get dark, I made my way back to the shack we were living in. I was still quite far away when I heard the shots—machine-gun blasts. I started to run. It was like one of those dreams, you know, where you run and run and never seem to move. I got there just in time to see a jeep roar off into the jungle. I couldn't even tell who they were, what side they were on."

Lenn stared out into the night for a dark, silent minute, then he continued, his voice harsher somehow. "When I walked into the house, there was blood everywhere. The two men she'd been caring for that day were drilled with bullet holes. I found Suzanna on the kitchen floor, holding her stomach." Lenn closed his eyes. "She was dead. Our baby was dead. And I think I died right along with them. The pain—the pain was too much. From that moment on, I made myself stop feeling. I swore I would never feel that deeply about anyone or anything ever again. I didn't want to let anyone get close to me. Not ever again."

Katie swiped the back of her hand across her face. The motion did little to stem the tears that were streaming down her cheeks. Now she knew. Knew why Lenn held into himself. Why he wouldn't let himself feel. Why he sometimes acted as if he didn't give a damn. And she grieved. For Lenn—and for herself.

For Lenn and the wife and child he had lost. For the friend he had lost, and for the innocence he could never regain. Now she knew why Lenn would never give himself again, and she grieved for herself.

Some small optimistic part of her had still hoped that her brother had been wrong. That Lenn himself had been wrong. That her own observations had been wrong. A stubborn streak of optimism had seen her through all those pranks of Lenn's, all that teasing, and allowed her to survive. Now as she stared out to sea, that optimism died.

Lenn gouged a piece out of his Styrofoam cup, then another, deliberately shredding the pieces smaller and smaller. "You know, Katie, sometimes I feel as if my whole life has been one royal screw-up. When I was a kid, I used to tug up my belt, stick out my chest, and strut around town like I owned it. I had the world by the tail, and once in a while I'd give it a good hard yank to let it know who was running the show. I should have known that one day reality would give me a good hard slap in the face and show me that the world didn't revolve around Lenn Domina after all." Lenn shoved the mangled cup into a pile on the blanket. "The hardest lesson I've ever learned was that we humans have damn little control over our lives."

She managed a tiny, rueful smile. "You've got a point there." Boy, did he ever have a point.

Suddenly, Lenn popped to his feet. "Hey, I didn't bring you to Cardiff to listen to my griping. We're getting all depressed here." He pulled her to her feet and flicked a tear from her cheek with his thumb. "Come on, let's go for a stroll and blow off the cobwebs."

Tucking Katie beneath his arm, Lenn steered her down the beach. He'd seen the pain he'd put in her eyes and ached for it, but he knew that if he and Katie were ever to have a chance, he had to let go of Suzanna. In talking about her, he finally felt he had. He looked down at the tumble of red curls that were riffling in the night breeze. He wanted to tell Katie how much he loved her. But the time wasn't right. They were both too down right now. He gazed out at the ocean. The night was so beautiful, maybe it could lift them out of their melancholy.

Lenn watched the moon dance over the waves in long, silver streams. A little way up the beach, a small group of people still in bathing suits gathered around a fire. They were playing guitars, singing and generally living it up. As he and Katie strolled by, they broke into a rock and roll version of "You Are My Sunshine." Lenn smiled as he and Katie paused for a minute to listen, feeling unaccountably better somehow when they turned back down the beach after the song was done. The tide was high, and the water lapped around their knees in places, drenching their jeans nearly to their thighs.

In front of their cabin, he turned Katie toward him, both of them bracing their feet in the flooded, yielding sand to steady themselves against the force of the water. He bent his head, found her mouth, and kissed her with all the tenderness that had been welling inside his soul.

Katie sank into his kiss, melting against the long, hard length of him. His shirt was a thin white cotton, and she could feel the warmth and contours of his body straining to fit with hers. He lifted his mouth, creating a distance between them so he could take her face between his hands. Gazing steadily into her eyes for a long, emotionally charged moment, he said in a low voice, "Thank you."

"W-what?" Katie peered up at him in a haze.

"Thank you for being a persistent, pesky little pain in the butt." He smiled indulgently down at her. "You made me face a lot of things I needed to. You'll never know how much you've done for me."

Katie felt a shaft of pain slash through her. She didn't want gratitude. And yet, swallowing to contain the ache in her heart, she knew that if it was all she would get from Lenn, she would take it while she could. She leaned against his side as they turned toward the motel.

Inside, dancing red flickers warmed the walls. The fire they had built earlier crackled quietly in the fireplace, spreading a golden glow on the fur stretched out on the hearth. Lenn led her to stand on the rug. Her bare toes curled into the tickling hairs.

"I need you, Katie." He brushed his thumb along her cheek, down across her mouth. "I want you."

Need. Want. Gratitude. Oh, God, it wasn't enough, but it would have to be. She reached out a hand and undid the one button that was holding Lenn's shirt together. Sliding the soft white cotton aside, she pressed her lips to the beaded male bud nestled in the dark swirls of hair covering his chest. She loved this man. It would have to be enough.

Lenn returned the favor, peeling her blouse from her body and letting it flutter to the floor. His mouth laved her peaking nipple as they both sank to their knees on the soft gray fur. She watched the hot play of red and gold along the curve of her breast, watched the slick glittering trail left as Lenn's tongue tasted the reflected flames that fluttered across her body, and she forgot everything but the burning sensations radiating everywhere he touched.

When he moved over her, she accepted him, accepted him and all he could give. And he gave her the stars.

In the afterglow, they lay curled in front of the dying fire, Lenn's finger tracing a softly tingling path along her naked, sated flesh.

"I love you."

Katie stiffened. "You don't have to say that." She didn't want empty words. Didn't want lies. He'd told her not more than a couple of hours ago how he would never love again. Did he think she'd forgotten?

"What do you mean? I don't *have* to say that. Of course, I have to say it. I love you, Katie."

"Lenn, don't." Katie rolled away and grabbed for her blouse, shrugging off Lenn's arm as she struggled into it. Jerking to a stand, she hopped on one foot then the other, pulling on her jeans.

Lenn bounded to his feet, magnificently naked in the fireglow, not bothering to gather his own clothes. "What the hell's got into you. I tell you I love you and you say *Don't, Lenn*. That's not exactly what I expected to hear."

He knew. Oh, God, he knew. He'd obviously expected her to return his declaration. That meant he knew she loved him, and he had tried to placate her by saying what he had. "Damn it, Lenn, I don't want words you don't mean. I can't handle that."

Lenn shook his head. "You think I'm snowing you? I don't believe this. I spill my guts to you, thinking that all those solicitous words meant you cared."

"Lenn, I—"

"Hell, *I* was the one being snowed, wasn't I?"

Bitterness tinged his voice. "All I was doing was appeasing that damned curiosity. How could I have been so stupid?" Lenn bent in one angry arc and scooped up his clothes. He stopped halfway to the bedroom door. "Or was it a payback? Did you suck me in? Get me to care then slap me down to get back for those childish pranks that you never seemed to be able to forgive? Well, Katie," his black stare cut through to her soul, "you did a damned good job."

For one foolish second, Katie wanted to race into the bedroom after him. Tell him he was wrong. But then she remembered. Remembered how adept Lenn was at turning things around so that the blame wasn't on him. That's what he was doing now. In fact, she'd bet he was pulling the angry, injured act as an easy out. He'd gotten her into his bed and now he needed a way to end it. And she'd played right into his hands.

Well, it wasn't any more than she'd expected. But why did it have to hurt so much? She looked around the firelit room. There wasn't even anything she could pick up and throw. And oh, how she wanted to throw something. To break something and see it smash into smithereens. The way her heart had.

She heard drawers slam and the strident scrape of hangers against the closet rod. Lenn stalked back into the room with his suitcase in hand. "You've got five minutes to get your stuff together while I check out. Five minutes. *Capisce*? Or I leave without you." He slammed out of the unit.

She was ready in four. And when she unpacked the jumble of her suitcase after the longest, most tension-filled ride of her life, she found the only thing she had missed was the plastic packet of birth-control pills that were still sitting in the medicine cabinet of the motel in Cardiff.

ELEVEN

Sal called approximately five times a day over the next two weeks. According to his woeful pleas, the photographer she'd talked into taking her place wasn't working out, and Lenn was acting like a bear with a sore tooth. Wouldn't she please come back?

Katie politely declined. Just as she, equally politely, informed her father that nothing was wrong the corresponding number of times a day he called. There was something in their voices when they talked to her. Something beneath their obvious concern. Actually, they sounded as if they felt kind of . . . guilty?

Well, they should. It was their fault she was facing the most desolate time of her life. They had talked her into that stupid job in the first place. She had told them she'd never be able to get along with Lenn Domina, and did they believe her? *Nooo*. But she had been right.

She had to stop thinking about Lenn. But how?

Everything seemed to revolve around her feelings for him. She tried keeping busy, doing other things, losing herself in her photography as she had done so often in the past. But nothing was any fun anymore. Even taking pictures had lost its appeal. Whenever she lined up a shot, the trees seemed to droop; the colors were dull and flat. Loneliness was everywhere. Even the birds sang with a little less zeal.

The phone started ringing. Katie snatched up her camera and charged out the door. She didn't want to talk to anyone. Not Sal, not her father, and especially not her mother. She didn't need to hear the sympathy that oozed in her mother's voice these days. What she needed was a nice stroll in the park around the corner.

The park was relatively empty at that time of the day, and she wandered aimlessly until she came to the children's playground. Aiming her camera at some laughing children playing on the swings, she tried to compose a photograph, but their joyful glee sent such a shaft of pain into her soul that she couldn't make her fingers press the release. Turning, she ran until the playground was out of sight, until she found an empty stretch of grass. With an anguished moan, she collapsed beneath a tree and cried. There, alone with the pigeons and the discarded candy wrappers flying in the breeze, she sobbed until there were no tears left to cry. Finally she drew a shaky breath and held it while she wiped her face on her sleeve, then let it out slowly. Propping her chin on her knees, she circled her legs with her arms and stared out across the park.

She'd been wrong. So very wrong, and she knew

it now. Over the last two weeks, her mind had replayed the weekend in Cardiff, and she realized she'd blown it. Lenn had given her a very private, very painful part of himself, and she had let her insecurities and her perception of his reputation destroy what might have been her one chance at finding something with the man she loved. And now he hated her. The scathing good-bye he had growled out when he dropped her at her apartment that night told her that much. Lenn had made it pretty clear he never wanted to see her again, and it was her own fault.

A hand settled on her shoulder and her heart stopped. She twisted around. Her eyes locked on a long pair of denim-clad legs, then traveled up to a bulky jean jacket to meet a pair of—blue eyes.

She swallowed her disappointment. "Hi, Chris. What are you doing here?"

"Tracking down my favorite sister. You weren't at your place, so I thought I'd give the park a shot before I gave up." He flopped down beside her. "Just another example of my brilliant deductive powers."

Katie managed a wan smile.

"So, how's it going, kid?" Chris leaned back on an elbow.

She shrugged listlessly. "Okay, I guess."

"You don't look okay. You look like you've dropped some weight."

"Some." But who cared.

"Want to talk about it?"

She threw a suspicious glance over her shoulder. "Dad send you?"

"Not exactly." Chris concentrated on the blade of grass he was twisting between his fingers. "He just told me he was concerned about you. Looks like he might have had reason. Got anything to do with the fact that you're not working for Sal anymore?''

Katie shrugged.

"Is it Domina? Damn it, Katie, I told you not to get mixed up with him.''

"No, it wasn't like that," she hastened to explain. "I was the one who screwed up. It was all my own fault."

Chris looked at her intently before asking softly, "What happened?"

Katie met her brother's troubled blue eyes and remembered all the times she'd run to him when she was hurt, remembered how he had stopped what he was doing to bandage a scraped knee or listen to an excited story—or a woeful one. Chris might bedevil her more than she liked, but she'd always been able to talk to him. She heaved a resigned sigh and poured out the story of her weekend. Finishing through quivering lips, she added, "He said he loved me. And, Chris, all I could think of was those stories I'd heard and all the times you told me how he'd never stick to one woman. I rejected him, and now he hates me. He has every right to hate me."

"Let me get this straight. Lenn told you about what happened in Nicaragua, about his wife?" Chris asked incredulously.

Katie nodded. "You knew?"

"Yeah, we went on a bender once a couple of years ago. Lenn got really down in his cups and told me the whole thing. That's why I knew he'd never take any woman seriously again." He plucked another blade of grass and stared at it for a while. "But I'm beginning to think I was wrong. Since then, I've gotten used to seeing the smooth-talking guy who cruised bars with me. Women would lean all over him, their boobs spilling into his beer, and he'd throw a wink over their heads and we'd laugh. He never went home alone, and he rarely saw the same woman twice.''

"Damn it, Chris, I don't want to hear about his other women, all right?''

"Hey, I didn't mean . . . The point I'm trying to make is that maybe with all that carousing around we did, I forgot the friend underneath the playboy, the man who spilled his guts to me that day. Forgot that he was a caring man who was blocking off that caring because it hurt too much. Maybe all he needed was someone to break down the wall he'd built. And it sounds to me that you might have managed to do that. Because, Katie, not once did I ever hear him tell one of the women he went out with that he loved her. That's not Lenn. He would never pretend just to make a score. If he told you he loved you, then I have to believe he meant it.''

"That might have been true at the time, but I threw it away. I hurt him when I wouldn't believe him.'' She buried her head in her hands. "Oh, Chris, what am I going to do? I feel so lost.''

"Call him. Talk to him. Because if I know Lenn and that damned Italian pride of his, he won't come to you, even if he does love you. And Katie, I think he does.''

Katie straightened and gazed at him through misty eyes. "You think so, Chris? You really think so?''

"Yeah, I do. He trusted you enough to tell you about Suzanna. That's got to mean a hell of a lot. He had to be stoned out of his gourd to tell *me*, and we've been friends since we were kids. It's not something that would come easy to him. Listen, I steered you wrong about Lenn before, and right now I regret nothing as much as I regret that, but this time, I know I'm right. Call him.''

Call him. Easier said than done. Katie must have picked up the phone ten times that evening, but every time she got to the last couple of digits of Lenn's number, she chickened out.

About nine-thirty she headed toward the phone again. This time she completed the series of numbers she intended to call.

"Sal, hi. It's Katie." She smiled at his exuberant hello. "Yeah, I'm fine. Listen, Sal, any chance of getting my job back?"

Katie stood with one hand holding open the swinging door and glanced around the newsroom. It hadn't changed. She made herself look over at Lenn's desk. It was empty. He wasn't here yet. She felt a surge of relief and wondered if this was such a good idea. It had seemed like one last night. She'd been so wary about calling Lenn, afraid he would hang up the minute he heard her voice, that she figured if she just showed up at work, he'd be forced to be at least civil. That might give her a chance to talk to him. To make things right. She squared her shoulders and stepped into the bustling office.

"Hey, Katie, good to see you back."

"You back for good?"

Questions and greetings came from all directions. She nodded and smiled, but she didn't really know the answers. A lot depended on Lenn.

Her desk was still there. Three feet from Lenn's. She sat behind it and waited. For excruciatingly long minutes. And the longer she waited, the crazier she got. Jumping up, she decided to see what was doing in the darkroom.

She was hiding. And she knew it. She sorted through cupboards, taking stock of what was in them even though she knew exactly. Things hadn't changed all that much in two weeks, except that somebody had left a stack of developing reels scattered on the counter. Neatness wasn't usually her strong suit, but today for some reason the untidy pile irritated her. She gathered the metal spools into her arms to transport them across the room to where they belonged.

The door slammed open. "You in here, Ballard?"

At the sound of the familiar voice, Katie spun with a jerk, dropping her armload. Reels went skittering and rolling across the floor.

"Katie?" Lenn bent automatically to pick up a spool that went spinning by his foot, grabbing up two more while he was at it. Straightening, he asked, "You're back?"

Katie nodded hesitantly.

He stared at her for a long minute, his eyes unreadable, and Katie felt her stomach churn. She was ready to turn and run when he bent to scoop up the other three reels she had dropped. He held them out toward her. She stared at them dimly.

"Here's your stuff."

"Oh, of course. Thanks." She felt like a total pinhead. Reaching for the reels, she noticed that his hand was shaking as badly as hers was. That made her feel a small measure better. She dropped the spools on the counter. Right where they'd been before she'd decided to move them.

"How've you been?" he asked.

Lonely. Miserable. "Fine. You?"

He shrugged, stuffing his thumbs in his pockets. "Getting by. You look like you've lost weight."

"Seven and a half pounds." Which, for the first time, made her feel good. *At least now*, she thought, *I can compete with your skinny-minnie-millers.* "What do you think?" Okay, so she was fishing.

He stole a quick glance down the length of her body. "I liked you better the way you were before. I've grown to appreciate a little meat with my potatoes."

Her heart did a small flip-flop. She'd put it all back on. For lunch, she'd eat the biggest, juiciest, most calorie-packed meal she could find.

"The guys kinda missed you around the newsroom."

What about you? Did you miss me? "That's nice. I kind of missed being here."

"You know, you didn't need to quit because of, uh, what happened between us." Lenn balanced on his heels.

"I thought it was the right thing to do." She picked right up at the word *us*. It made her feel hopeful.

They stared at each other in silence. She searched her addled mind for something to talk about. "You trying to grow a beard?"

Frowning, he touched his shadowed chin, as if it came as a surprise that there were whiskers growing there. "Nah, I guess I just haven't bothered to shave for a couple of days."

Everything went quiet again. Katie bit her tongue to keep from babbling a whole bunch of nonsense. She couldn't think of where to begin. How to tell him she was sorry. "I missed you, Lenn."

He looked at her a long while, then asked, "Why?"

He wasn't going to make it easy for her. But then, she'd realized this week that very little in life *was* easy. Sometimes a person has to take a chance.

"Because . . . because I love you."

"Why?"

Why? Why? What on earth was wrong with this guy? He sounded like a little kid playing Pester Mommy. Didn't he know she was eating crow. Apologizing, for Pete's sake. "Why? Damn it, Domina, how should I know? I just do," she shouted, then clamped her hand over her mouth. Oh, God, she'd blown it again. Lenn pivoted on a heel and headed for the door.

"Lenn, I—"

He clicked the lock and flicked on the safelight that would alert anyone outside that developing was in progress. Turning, he leaned back against the wall in the soft red glow that filled the room. Katie held her breath.

"You know ever since that first day when I found you in here bathed in this erotic lighting, I've had this . . . well, kind of a fantasy."

Erotic? What on earth was erotic about a safelight, for crying out loud? "Lenn, what are you doing? I just told you I love you, and you're acting like some kind of nutcase. That's not—"

"What you expected?"

"No, I mean yes, I mean . . ." Damn him, he

was throwing her own words back at her. "Lenn, I—"

"You expected me to gladly tell you I love you again. Okay, I do. Take off your jeans."

"What?" Katie felt her heart take wing. "You love me?"

"Of course I do. I told you that. Why are your jeans still on?" He shoved away from the wall. "That first day you were wearing a short little nothing of a skirt. I'll bet your blouse'll be just about as long."

Katie backed against the counter, finally realizing where Lenn's thoughts were headed. "Lenn, we can't, I mean—"

"Why can't we?" He stalked closer.

"Because we're at work." Only, all of a sudden, it didn't feel like that anymore. The room and the lighting that were an automatic, mundane part of her workday had insanely taken on the erotic cast that Lenn had talked about. "Wh-what will people think?"

Hot red color washed over Lenn's skin, over the white cotton shirt he was slowly unbuttoning, over those tight jeans he was wearing, and a corresponding heat rushed to every vital part of her body.

"They'll think you're developing something. The jeans, Katie," he sent her a look that could have melted the polar caps, "and whatever's underneath, too."

As if he controlled her with some kind of marionette strings, Katie toed off her shoes and slid her jeans and panties off in one long, slow slither, leaving the whole pile in lump on the floor. Her eyes never once left his.

"You know, you've got incredibly long, gorgeous

legs for such a bit of a thing," he said softly, his eyes gleaming in appreciation.

He didn't even have to touch her, and she was liquid, ready for him. He crossed the room slowly, deliberately, and lifted her against the sink, propping her so she was balanced with her feet just inches off the floor. "Just the right height," he murmured as he stepped between her legs and took her mouth.

She slid her hands between them and fumbled with his zipper, finally releasing him to her waiting warmth. With one quick thrust they were joined. His tongue wrestled with hers, twining, tasting as he moved within her, fast and hard, taking her high, so high that she cried out her pleasure, his mouth swallowing her moan of fulfillment.

Spent and clinging together, they nibbled and nicked at each other, sipping and savoring the floating parachute ride back to earth.

Katie sunk her too-heavy head into the comfortable crook of Lenn's neck. "Wow."

"Oh, God, Red, I love you. I want you. I need you, and I'm going to do everything in my power to convince you I mean what I say."

"Oh, Lenn." Her arms still wrapped around his neck, Katie leaned back to look into his face. "You don't have to. I was the one who acted like a fool. I listened to everyone but you, and you were the only one who said what counted."

"You believe I love you?"

She nodded.

"Oh, Katie." He covered her lips softly, tasting gently at first, then with more force, more passion, and she felt him stir between her legs.

"Uh uh, you lethal little witch. No way." Lenn

backed away, awkwardly pulled his jeans together, then painfully, it appeared, did up his zipper. "Next time's going to be slow and easy—and long." He lifted her to the floor. "Get dressed. We're taking the rest of the day off. Someone else can cover the news today."

Katie scrambled into her panties, only a little self-consciously. Somehow having Lenn watch her dress didn't seem so strange now. She was cramming her second leg into her jeans when Lenn said softly, "Marry me, Katie."

Nearly overbalancing in shock she yanked her jeans to her hips. "What?" She glared at him, her fly gaping open.

"Marry me and give me a home."

"Oh, yes. Oh, God, yes." She stumbled across the two feet into his arms.

Lenn grinned at her. "When? How about this afternoon. In Las Vegas. We could—"

Katie pressed a hand to his lips. "No, Lenn, not like that. Let's do this right. With your family and my family. I want to look back on our wedding day and have a whole bunch of memories. Not some lickety-split job. I want one of those big Italian weddings I've heard so much about."

"But you're Irish."

"Well, then, an Irish-Italian wedding."

"All right, whatever it takes, because I intend to spend the rest of my life making you happy."

"Lenn, uh . . ." She didn't know how to say it, but she needed to know. "About, well, about your wandering. I don't know if I—"

"Want a husband who gads about the world? I told you I'd come home to settle a few things. Well, one of those things was to make amends with Sal, and I have. In fact, I think the alienation I felt around my family was part of why I kept away. Why I traveled and didn't stay. But I also came home looking for some kind of peace, because I was tired of the aimless life I was living. I found that peace in you.'' He kissed her with all the tender passion she could ever want, then said, "Now zip up. I've got a big lonely bed that needs an afternoon of activity to make it feel useful.''

Katie quickly complied, listening with a contented smile while Lenn called Sal and informed him that he and his photographer were taking the afternoon off. She could still hear Sal's shout of blustering outrage bellowing through the receiver that Lenn laid on the darkroom counter as they sneaked down the hall and out of the building.

Two months later, Katie had the big Italian wedding she wanted. The whole event, ceremony and all, took place in the Dominas' backyard, the only place large enough to hold the many relatives of both the O'Brien and Domina families. Located on the crest of a hill in the San Fernando valley, the Dominas' adobe home was a smaller, whiter version of an old Spanish alcazar set amid an acre of plush green lawn.

Set up behind the house on this glorious day were several long tables dressed in brilliant white table-cloths with crisp corners rippling in the breeze. On the tables were vases of assorted wildflowers because that's what Katie wanted. They were, she mused, somehow symbolic of her relationship with Lenn. Two thorny wildflowers struggling in a world where poise, perfection, and *normalcy* were high in demand.

And there was food. More food than could possibly be consumed by the hundred and fifty or so guests present, of whom only a handful were Katie's friends and family. The rest were Lenn's. Brothers, sisters, uncles, aunts, grandparents, cousins, nieces, nephews, cousins of cousins, and even, Katie suspected, hairdressers of cousins.

There was laughter and music aplenty. A small band played under a multicolored awning, and wine flowed from a seemingly endless source. Two groups had joined hands and were dancing in two circles, one going clockwise and one counterclockwise. Others applauded them on while small furry dogs yipped at their heels.

Katie surveyed the scene from a large balcony. She spotted Lenn standing at one of the tables, feeding his face and chatting with a group of men. *Her husband*. The sight of him did crazy, wonderful things to her heart. He looked like a gleaming knight in his white suit. All he needed was the horse. Feeling incredibly smug, she turned and wandered into the house to find a bathroom. After a round of dancing with vigorous uncles, she was distinctly sticky and needed to freshen up. Heading down a long hall, she stopped in her tracks when she heard her father's voice behind one of the closed doors.

"Well, we did it, Sal. It worked like a charm and they're none the wiser. But I'll have to admit, it was touch and go for a while."

She told herself it was rude to eavesdrop and took a step away, but Sal's reply drew her back like a magnet.

"Yeah, throwing them together like that was kind of risky. Both of them are so pigheaded. Having them work together was a brilliant idea, Charlie. Brilliant."

"The sparks sure did fly, didn't they?" Charlie replied with a hearty chuckle.

Sal's answering laugh was a continuous sort of hissing sound. "Sparks. It was more like blowtorches. That daughter of yours had my boy in knots. Walked around for days with his head hanging between his legs like a lovesick schoolboy. Felt sorry for him for a while—but what an ending."

"I knew they'd hit it off." Charlie said I-told-you-so in his own sneaky way. "Remember a couple of years ago when Lenn was in town and I suggested fixing him up with Katie and you said, *Nah, it'll never work*. You said, *Lenny's too independent to put up with her temper*. You said . . ."

Katie shook her head and walked away, knowing she should be mad as hell at both of them. Butch Cassidy and the Sundance Kid had been at it again. But today she was too happy to care.

Scrunching her voluminous skirt to her sides, she squeezed through the bathroom door and leaned against it. The old reprobates had actually done something right for once. She grinned into the mirror.

"Katie? Hey, Katie, where are you?" Lenn's voice called down the hall.

Katie cracked open the door and poked her head through. Lenn furtively glanced both ways then ducked into the bathroom with her. She could tell by the silly smile on his face that he'd had more than his share of the free-flowing wine.

"Hey, wife. Wanna make out?" He backed her up against a wall, his eyes glinting with that hint of devil she had come to love.

"Lenn, are you crazy?" She felt the heavy folds of her dress being pulled up.

"Are you in there?" Lenn fumbled with the yards of lace and satin.

Chuckling happily, Katie whispered, "Le-enn."

"Aha, there you are." His searching hand found the band of her silky white panty hose and slipped them down her legs.

"I want you, Katie. Here. Now." He had a silly grin on his face, but she could tell he was dead serious.

"You got a fetish about rooms with sinks?"

Lenn waggled his eyebrows, and she could tell he was remembering that day in the darkroom. "You bet." He burrowed his head into the crook of her neck, and she caught a tiny whiff of wine mingling with the heady smell that belonged to Lenn alone. "What I really have a fetish for is sexy little red-heads in white.

Nibbling a shivering trail along the curve of her shoulder, he made another foray under her skirt and stripped her panties off. She heard the rasp of a zipper just before he pinned her to the wall and hoisted her legs up around his hips.

Half laughing, half overcome with passion, she hissed, "Lenn, someone will hear us!"

"So what if someone hears? We're married," he breathed. Pulling back to gaze hotly into her eyes, he groaned, "God, I love you," and plunged deep inside her.

Out in the hall, Sal Domina put one hand on the knob, while the other started unbuckling his belt.

"Lenn, ooh, Lenn, that feels . . ."

Sal jerked his hand from the knob as if it were red hot. *Kids these days!* Shaking his head, he headed back down the hall. It was a good thing this house had other bathrooms. This one was bound to be occupied for some time.

SHARE THE FUN . . .
SHARE YOUR NEW-FOUND TREASURE!!

You don't want to let your new books out of your sight?
That's okay. Your friends can get their own. Order below.

No. 152 PERSISTENCE PAYS by Kristal Ryan
Katie's all-time nemesis returns to drive her crazy—crazy with passion.

No. 36 DADDY'S GIRL by Janice Kaiser
Slade wants more than Andrea is willing to give. Who wins?

No. 37 ROSES by Caitlin Randall
It's an inside job & K.C. helps Brett find more than the thief!

No. 38 HEARTS COLLIDE by Ann Patrick
Matthew finds big trouble and it's spelled P-a-u-l-a.

No. 40 CATCH A RISING STAR by Laura Phillips
Justin is seeking fame; Beth helps him find something more important.

No. 41 SPIDER'S WEB by Allie Jordan
Silvia's quiet life explodes when Fletcher shows up on her doorstep.

No. 43 DUET by Patricia Collinge
Adam & Marina fit together like two perfect parts of a puzzle!

No. 44 DEADLY COINCIDENCE by Denise Richards
J.D.'s instincts tell him he's not wrong; Laurie's heart says trust him.

No. 46 ONE ON ONE by JoAnn Barbour
Vincent's no saint but Loie's attracted to the devil in him anyway.

No. 47 STERLING'S REASONS by Joey Light
Joe is running from his conscience; Sterling helps him find peace.

No. 48 SNOW SOUNDS by Heather Williams
In the quiet of the mountain, Tanner and Melaine find each other again.

No. 51 RISKY BUSINESS by Jane Kidwell
Blair goes undercover but finds more than she bargained for with Logan.

No. 54 DAYDREAMS by Marina Palmieri
Kathy's life is far from a fairy tale. Is Jake her Prince Charming?

No. 55 A FOREVER MAN by Sally Falcon
Max is trouble and Sandi wants no part of him. She *must* resist!

No. 56 A QUESTION OF VIRTUE by Carolyn Davidson
Neither Sara nor Cal can ignore their almost magical attraction.

No. 57 BACK IN HIS ARMS by Becky Barker
Fate takes over when Tara shows up on Rand's doorstep again.

No. 59 **13 DAYS OF LUCK** by Lacey Dancer
Author Pippa Weldon finds her real-life hero in Joshua Luck.

No. 60 **SARA'S ANGEL** by Sharon Sala
Sara *must* get to Hawk. He's the only one who can help.

No. 61 **HOME FIELD ADVANTAGE** by Janice Bartlett
Marian shows John there is more to life than just professional sports.

No. 62 **FOR SERVICES RENDERED** by Ann Patrick
Nick's life is in perfect order until he meets Claire!

No. 63 **WHERE THERE'S A WILL** by Leanne Banks
Chelsea goes toe-to-toe with her new, unhappy business partner.

No. 64 **YESTERDAY'S FANTASY** by Pamela Macaluso
Melissa always had a crush on Morgan. Maybe dreams do come true!

No. 65 **TO CATCH A LORELEI** by Phyllis Houseman
Lorelei sets a trap for Daniel but gets caught in it herself.

No. 66 **BACK OF BEYOND** by Shirley Faye
Dani and Jesse are forced to face their true feelings for each other.

- -

Meteor Publishing Corporation
Dept. 693, P. O. Box 41820, Philadelphia, PA 19101-9828

Please send the books I've indicated below. Check or money order (U.S. Dollars only)—no cash, stamps or C.O.D.s (PA residents, add 6% sales tax). I am enclosing $2.95 plus 75¢ handling fee for *each* book ordered.

Total Amount Enclosed: $_____.

—— No. 152	—— No. 43	—— No. 54	—— No. 61
—— No. 36	—— No. 44	—— No. 55	—— No. 62
—— No. 37	—— No. 46	—— No. 56	—— No. 63
—— No. 38	—— No. 47	—— No. 57	—— No. 64
—— No. 40	—— No. 48	—— No. 59	—— No. 65
—— No. 41	—— No. 51	—— No. 60	—— No. 66

Please Print:
Name _____

Address _____ Apt. No. _____

City/State _____ Zip _____

Allow four to six weeks for delivery. Quantities limited.